Dedalus Euro Shorts
General Editor: Timothy Lane

Lobster

Guillaume Lecasble

$\mathscr{L}$*obster*

Translated by Polly McLean

Dedalus

Supported using public funding by
ARTS COUNCIL
ENGLAND

Published in the UK by Dedalus Limited,
24-26, St Judith's Lane, Sawtry, Cambs, PE28 5XE
email: info@dedalusbooks.com
www.dedalusbooks.com

ISBN printed book 978 1 915568 23 6
ISBN ebook 978 1 915568 24 3

Dedalus is distributed in the USA & Canada by SCB Distributors,
15608 South New Century Drive, Gardena, CA 90248
email: info@scbdistributors.com   www.scbdistributors.com

Dedalus is distributed in Australia by Peribo Pty Ltd.
58, Beaumont Road, Mount Kuring-gai, N.S.W 2080
email: info@peribo.com.au

First Published in France in 2003
First published by Dedalus in 2005, new edition in 2023

Printed by Clays Ltd, Elcograf S.p.A.
Typeset by RefineCatch Ltd, Bungay, Suffolk

A CIP Catalogue record for this book is available from the British Library

THE AUTHOR

Guillaume Lecasble was born in 1954. He started painting at the age of nineteen and had a first solo exhibition eleven years later. From his artwork – and particularly the portrait of a chorus of monks – he became inspired to experiment with new approaches to film-making. Various short films yielded a pair of characters, *bonhomme & bonfemme*, who then reincarnated themselves in a series of highly praised books for children. Painting continues to inspire and accompany his written and cinematographic work. *Lobster*, his first novel, was published to critical acclaim in France in 2003. His second novel, *Cut*, was published in 2004.

THE TRANSLATOR

Polly McLean grew up in Paris and Oxford. She is a freelance translator whose latest credits include a novel by Yasmina Traboulsi for Blackamber Books, and a history of that well-known liberal agreement, the Entente Cordiale.

Dedalus Euro Shorts

Dedalus Euro Shorts is a series of short European fiction which can be read from cover to cover on Euro Star or on a short flight.

Titles currently available are :

Helena, or the Sea in Summer – Julian Ayesta
My Little Husband – Pascal Bruckner
An Afternoon with Rock Hudson – Mercedes Deambrosis
The Prodigious Physician – Jorge de Sena
Cleopatra goes to Prison – Claudia Durastanti
Ink in the Blood – Stéphane Hochet
Alice, the Sausage – Sophie Jabès
Las Adventures des Inspector Cabillot – Diego Marani
The Staff Room – Markus Orths
On the Run – Martin Prinz

Lobster didn't want to go. He put up a fight. The fisherman grabbed him by the tail and pulled him out of the pot. Tied his pincers. Threw him into a crate on top of the other lobsters. His shell stank of contact with human hands. Lobster's mum and dad were also aboard. He thought of his brother. Remembered the smell of rotting fish in the water the day he'd disappeared. The same smell of bloody fish heads that had enticed Lobster and all the others into these death crates.

The crate was full. The fishermen covered their catch with a thick layer of fresh seaweed. Nailed down the lid. Only rays of light came through the planks. The lobsters could see nothing of the outside. They were all terrified, and so squashed they were unable to move. They could hear the trawler creaking. Voices shouting to make themselves heard over the spray. The sea was raging. The wind bent the poles on the buoys, submerging the flags on the lobster pots. This was Lobster and his companions' first experience of the rolling sea. Quite different from the deep currents. They all felt sick – and that's without counting the human stink.

The rolling calmed. The voices returned. The crates were unloaded and stacked on top of each other. For the first time, the lobsters heard the sound of hooves on cobblestones, clay and gravel. For the first time, they smelled the fragrances of rural spring: fruit trees in blossom, luxuriant wet grass, and lily of the valley, early that year. Then the cobblestones again. Voices. Shouts. The iron wheels came to a halt, silent now.

The lobsters were unloaded, transported. They discovered the metallic music of kitchen utensils. Then other voices, new shouts. The lids were taken off. Some of the lobsters hadn't survived the slow suffocation of their dry journey. The rest were tipped into aquariums – huge, unbelievably luxurious aquariums, with special pebbles and exotic marine plants. The water was salty. It had no smell. Dead water. Slowly Lobster and the others began moving again. Crashed into the glass, unable to understand the see-through wall. On the other side was a large dining room.

When the lights were switched on those able to see clearly in the dark were blinded. Slowly, things came into focus. It was very busy – table-cloths were being smoothed, plates and glasses arranged, chairs set out, tables dragged across the floor. Flowers were being displayed, wine decanted, bread put in baskets. More lights came on. People were coming down the elegant stair-case, sitting down, appraising each other, looking across to other tables. The women were richly attired. The men all looked exactly the same, dressed in black and white. Once they'd read the menu, some of them got up and walked to the aquarium with the head waiter. To start with they walked round it, getting all excited as they pointed at a particular lobster, laughing, teasing each other, and most of all, salivating ... Lobster sensed their increasing appetite, unable to believe what he saw in their shining eyes. A woman

11

pushed her nose right up to the glass – so close that some of her face powder remained. A very young woman, Angelina, picked out Lobster's dad. The head waiter used a shrimping net to catch him. Lobster watched his father trying to escape from the net. His imprisoned silhouette stood out against the light of the chandeliers. Lobster wanted to rescue him, but his mother held him back – he mustn't draw attention to himself. The man shook the net over the aquarium to let the water drip off. Carried it through a white door with a big porthole.

Lobster and his mother looked at each other. They waved their feelers around, trying to intercept a signal. All they could pick up was the smell of bay leaves. It was new to them but reminiscent of certain kinds of seaweed. Then a scream! A brief scream, and silence. The white door with the porthole opened. A table on wheels emerged and Lobster recognised his father on a plate. His shell was red. His eyes were dead. Lobster thought of his brother. He must have ended up like this, along with all those who disappeared from the sea bed: boiled, with his claws folded back along his belly.

Lobster could see the head waiter serving Angelina. She was facing him. He watched: her every movement was intent on devouring his dad. He could hear the shell cracking, the clatter of stainless steel on china, hear her chewing, biting, sucking. An older man, Maurice, sat down at her table. With her mouth full, she nodded OK, sitting up straight and ordering dessert.

Lobster's mother was cooked two days later. The smell of bay leaves heralded the death, as it always did.

The next evening a little boy selected Lobster, thinking he was a toy. The head waiter fished him out. Dripped him dry. Took him off to the kitchen. The child didn't understand and burst into tears – he wanted another one. Lobster was on the way to the white door with the big porthole. He was frightened. More frightened than he had ever been. When the fishermen had taken him out of the sea, he hadn't known what to expect. Now he was going to a certain death. He tried to draw strength from his parents' example. But it didn't help – he was too afraid. He watched the polished shoes marching him towards death. The white door opened into white light. He saw how death comes about, how all living things go under the knife – and then into pots and pans. Fruit, vegetables, poultry, plants and animals alike are cut up, gutted, sliced, minced, carved, chopped; invariably ending up boiled, roasted, seared, burnt. Lobster the scavenger realised that in this world, you kill to eat.

At exactly the moment Lobster hit the boiling water, a massive jolt overturned the pot. The steaming stock spilled out leaving Lobster unconscious on the floor. The cooks fled, somehow not crushing him underfoot. A wave of freezing water from the gangway sent his contorted body swirling into the dining room. Only Angelina was still there, with Maurice on his knees at her feet. The cold had gripped his heart. Angelina was trying to lift him up. Maurice clutched hold of her ankle and collapsed. Then died. Knee-deep in water, bent over and shivering, Angelina tried to unclench the vice-like grip of his fingers. She managed only to soak the bodice of her dress, making her colder still. Held captive to

Maurice's five fingers, she fumed, "Here I am, about to die. And once again, I'm lumbered with a man!" Maurice had invited himself into her life on the first day of the voyage, following her around, eating when she ate, drinking when she drank, and endlessly promising her the world. She took no notice – his only value was as protection from the other passengers in search of romance aboard the *Titanic*.

Angelina had taken this ship because it was unsinkable. Her life seemed to founder more each day, and before dying she'd wanted to taste what it felt like to be certain for once of not going under. For the duration of the voyage she'd wanted to forget her despair – because, while she had done many things with men, she had never reached orgasm. Excess, vice and oblivion had led her to nothing but this sorry state. As soon as she boarded she hated herself for giving in to the pull of this arrogant feat of engineering, for doubting her determination to die. Now she was white with rage as she worked at Maurice's stubborn finger and thumb, her whole arm immersed in the freezing water. Maurice, ancient Maurice with his dodgy heart, dry skin and gnarled joints, was having the last laugh. And she'd thought he was the one who was weak, worn out by age and emotion.

Lobster comes to his senses. He can't understand it. His shell is red, which must mean they've killed him – but he's alive. Yet the bay leaf smell coming out of him is definitely a death smell. The same smell that accompanied the death of all his kinsfolk. It's how his father smelled, and his mother, when they went by in front of him with their shells red, plopped onto their backs with their claws folded rearwards.

Images start coming back to him – the simmering stock, the way his eyes were scalded by the steam, and of course that smell of bay leaves. After that it all goes black, right until his awakening in this cold salty seawater. Alive! He's got to accept that he's alive, despite his shell having the smell and colour of death.

Right in front of him, Angelina is bent over, her hands purple from the cold, trying to break Maurice's fingers. She's not getting anywhere.

Sudden death and freezing water have paralysed his sinews and fused his bones together. In one fluid movement she stands up, flicks back her tousled hair and pins it up with a brooch from her dress. Lobster recognises her, thinks "she's the one who ate my dad". Unknown feelings brew in him. Vengeance and desire make his flesh tingle in a way he's never felt before. He's attracted to this woman. He, a lobster, attracted to a woman. He comes closer, the better to see. The better to clarify this shocking situation. Angelina's beauty is enough to bring on fevers, and Lobster feels one mounting in him. His body heats up, but it doesn't stop his craving for vengeance. He doesn't know what to do – for the first time he is being forced to use his reason, rather than his instinct.

Angelina was so nervous, so frozen and exasperated by the stiffness of the corpse clutching at her life that she didn't notice Lobster's feelers brushing against her ankles. Although he was murmuring "she ate my dad", his gaze was already climbing the length of her legs, right up to the satin of her panties. The fabric was billowing around her cold-tensed buttocks. Pale downy hair stood up over goose bumps. "She ate my dad," he told himself again, "she ate my dad." It didn't stop these shimmering hints of fabric causing his whole body to flood with desire. He was bowled over by human flesh. Lobster was experiencing lust for a woman. "Has that scalding made me see the world from a human perspective?" he wondered. But who cared – this lust was a fact and he was starting to enjoy it. He was feeling desire for a shell-less body. A supple, soft, silky body. A body with no hard edges. He was feeling desire for flesh, for skin. This feeling overwhelmed him, decided him: he opened his pincers and snap! Cut through the wrist that had been imprisoning Angelina. Maurice's body floated away, taken by the current. Angelina thought she saw a little devil in the bloody water. She couldn't understand why the hand was still attached to her ankle. She crossed the dining room against the current, icy water up to her thighs, blood in her wake. She, who wanted to die. She just needed to lie down. But that hand was stopping her from escaping into death; it was pushing her towards life. She shivered. The cold had entered her body and her mind; she didn't know what to think of this severed hand. Had her will to live cut it off? Or was it a product of the madness rising in her with the cold?

She reached the staircase and climbed the first step but the cold was numbing her mind. She fainted, upright and motionless with seawater up to her belly. Lobster swam to her purple feet. Cut off the bloodless hand with his pincers, and climbed up the inside of the leg as far as the clenched knees. He was amazed at the pleasure he felt from being held in this way. His pincers slipped between the thighs, prising them gently apart. His feelers were just able to reach the satin of the panties. They fluttered, made the labia quiver. Under the shimmering material a hint of life was returning. Angelina's thighs relaxed. Lobster pulled back his feelers. Tensed and released his tail. His strokes were fast and powerful. He was making headway. He sank himself into her warming muscles; his tail did not falter. He moved forward, a centimetre at a time. Yes! Suddenly he could see the fabric clearly, glistening, pearl-like. He brought his pincers forward. Caught hold of the lace border. Pulled back the slippery satin and snipped right through it. The panties opened, the two separate pieces floating soft as seaweed in the swirl. The hair round the vulva was undulating. Lobster put his pincer in and closed it on the clitoris with the dexterity of a practised lover. What he did to Angelina next so warmed her insides that she returned to life, arching her back. Lobster was thrown into the air, stiffening his tail as he slapped back against the water in time with Angelina's rhythm. And so their wedding dance began: Angelina and Lobster at the foot of the elegant dining room staircase. Her creamy woman's body, convulsed with pleasure, trailing a bright red crustacean with one pincer secured in her hairs and the other working her clitoris, as they moved between air and water, water and air; the exuberance of these two bodies as the water spurted between her buttocks and surged around her thighs.

The bay leaf aroma embedded in Lobster's shell invigorated Angelina, returning her to consciousness. Her heat was triumphing over the cold water. Her thighs kept parting and closing. Lobster was dripping with vaginal juices. Angelina thrust more quickly, coming down rhythmically against the water. The foam around them was a glory to their union. Angelina arched her back, buttocks surging out of the water. Lobster, intimately attached to her, was shaken by staccato vibrations. Angelina reached orgasm for the first time in her life. Pleasure quivered under her nails and shook her jaw. Her toes felt connected to her throat. Unfamiliar sap was running right through her. Gently, her body relaxed and re-entered the water now warm from the fever of their union; Lobster floated motionless on his back with his pincers splayed.

Happily afloat on the swirl of the sinking ship, Angelina slipped a hand between her legs, picked up Lobster and put his head inside her mouth. She rolled her tongue around his eyes and mandibles. As Lobster was rinsed in saliva he dreamt of his new life – a pleasure to be re-lived again and again.

The sirens that had been wailing for an hour

brought Angelina back to the reality of the ship-wreck. She slipped Lobster between her breasts.

His shell felt rough – she loved the sensation of his little claws on her skin. She felt immortal. Bound-ing up the stairs two at a time, she reached the gangway where exhausted passengers were on the point of giving up. The shouting was full of hurry and panic, with men, women and children every-where; she went to her cabin. The soaked dress fell to her feet. Her panties were in shreds and her body covered in bruises. Lobster, lying motionless on the bed, watched her skin redden under the scalding shower. She never did like to leave the salt on her skin after being in the sea. Clasping Lobster to her naked body, she compared their redness, whispering, "look, we're the same now".

Angelina slipped Lobster into the pocket of her winter coat. The feel of his constantly moving legs gave her the courage to fight against her death wish.

She got into a lifeboat. Sat at the outside edge of the middle bench, couldn't help trying to touch the water. Her youthful radiance antagonised the grey woman next to her. Eyes, skin, teeth, soul – everything about her was grey. The bay leaf aroma annoyed her. She breathed out through her nose, PFFFT. Angelina was driving her crazy, trying to touch the water, behaving like a child, leaning over the gunwale at such a desperate time. Then Angelina's contortions made the pocket of her coat gape open. When she saw the red pincers, the grey woman shrieked in fear. Her shout ricocheted across the cold, calm water:

"A lobster, a lobster! Food, she's got food!"

Her voice, turned shrill by panic, paralysed the other passengers. Before Angelina could react, the woman was on her, trying to grab Lobster. Her hands had the strength of terror. Her dry fingers closed over Angelina's wrists, cutting off her ability to fight. The pocket was ripped; Lobster fell overboard. Angelina froze, stunned by the violence. The grey woman grabbed an oar, using it to slap splashily at the water, hitting Lobster on the head. Knocked unconscious, he sank like a stone. The grey woman sat down again, silently. Everyone was looking at her. Suddenly you could see the child she once was, squeezing her hands between her thighs, looking at her shoes. Her shoulders were hunched. Her neck had disappeared. Tears dripped onto her lifejacket.

Leaning over the water, Angelina was acutely aware of everything that had happened between her and him. Him, disappearing into the ocean. Ocean, engulfing the ship. Shipwreck, which in a single movement had allowed her to discover orgasm and was now taking away the source of her bliss. She gazed into the night. An abyss yawned inside her, expelling that essence of pleasure which sank with Lobster into the oblivion of the ocean depths. She had to find him again! A sailor seized the collar of her coat and grasped the leg already halfway overboard. Angelina was too weak to fight; she resigned herself for now.

Lobster was sinking. Slowly. Unconscious. In a halo of Angelina's tears.

As he sank deeper, he slowly regained consciousness. In pain, unable to move, sinking. Passengers, stiff from death and cold, sank with him. Towards the dark night of the deep, where the lobsters eat, see, procreate, live. Lobster felt fraternal as he looked at them. Sensitive to their tense faces, to the fear that showed through their open eyes. Sensitive to man, to humans. Yet his appetite stimulated by the feast these corpses would become. Lobster no longer knew what to think. Man or lobster, which was he?

Would he seek revenge for his parents' death by feasting on humans? His father and mother had been fished out of the water for their meal;

now, sinking, they were about to provide his own. Cosmic justice? Lobster didn't know any more; his body had kept its animal instinct but his mind had been taken over by human thoughts.

The *Titanic* was going under. The turbulent water tossed the victims around, creating macabre patterns. Lobster himself was sucked up in the current, pulled across the top deck, swept along the gangways at surprising speed, into an air pocket, down through empty space, landing in near still water. Here, women and men were holding each other by the hand, in a big circle, floating. They wore different expressions from the others: they hadn't fled from death. They'd waited for it. Looked it in the eye. Their hands, frozen by the cold, made the circle indestructible. Lobster was moved. His body, still painful, started to come back to life. He swam. From face to face. The old woman who ate his mother was there. Her face was the most serene of all.

"I'm going to eat you first," he said to himself, testing the firmness of her flesh with his pincers. "You know, soon it'll be swarming with crabs, lobsters, sea spiders – every kind of scavenger. I don't want you ending up in just anyone's claws. And afterwards, no matter how long it takes, I'm going to find Angelina."

Lying on her bed, Angelina could hear the floor-boards creaking under her father's weight, like when he used to come and put his ear to the door, listening to the silence. She was no longer a little girl, but she knew he was there anyway, hesitating, afraid to knock and come in. Pondering all the things he would have liked to say to her.

Angelina took her hand out of her coat pocket. The shipwreck coat. Sniffed the backs of her fingers; that bay leaf aroma, Lobster's smell.

Over the month that she'd been in New York, this gesture had become instinctual, repetitive, reassuring. She wore the coat only at home, didn't expose it to the kind of smoky dive she fre-quented. She kept a handkerchief in the pocket, to take with her when she went out.

Angelina listened to the creaking of the wooden floor. She could hear her father's sadness at knowing she was wrapped up in her coat, a clear sign that she still hadn't left the lifeboat. He wanted her to meet other survivors; he believed in the power of sharing. He was leaving for Long Island that night, to see Jennifer.

Angelina had spent every afternoon of the last week preparing for this evening. She'd even managed to get hold of the *Titanic* chef's recipe for stock.

As soon as she heard the front door close she leapt out of bed like a child. Checked, through the window; saw her father's slightly stooped back; took the coat off. Folded it, making sure the coat tails covered Lobster's pocket. To keep his smell in. Put an encyclopaedia on top. Just to be sure.

She went down to the kitchen. She'd bought a large pot. Her father had been intrigued – she'd never shown the slightest interest in that kind of thing. But then she'd been behaving so strangely since the shipwreck.

Angelina copied Rose Mary's routine. Put the

large empty pot on the hob. Filled it with several saucepans of water.

The ingredients for the stock had been ready since the day before. All she had to do now was wait. She dipped her finger in the water every minute. Watching the clock.

As arranged, the fishmonger's boy rang the doorbell at 10pm. Twelve lobsters rattling in a crate. The clenching of her cunt made Angelina squeeze her thighs together. She grabbed the crate, holding it against her belly to carry it. This meant she had to take small steps, but could feel the lobsters' activity. The delivery boy watched her go; she was usually so generous when he brought the fish. He shut the door and left.

The aroma of boiling stock filled the kitchen. Angelina grabbed the first lobster with a pair of wooden tongs. Plunged and removed the beast, quick as a slap in the face. But it was her first attempt at boiling a lobster. She hadn't reckoned on the tail whipping round; he got away, splashing her, scalding her skin through her blouse. Angelina was too tense to notice the pain. She threw the lobster into the sink. Unmoved by its suffering. She wanted *the* Lobster. He had touched her. This lobster, alive or dead, was nothing but a crustacean. With the second one, she tied the tail to the handle of a wooden spoon. Immersed the animal and pulled it out again. Unbelievable. Even she was shocked by its liveliness. The pink lobster was still fighting. Angelina turned her head away in self-protection. Its shell got more and more red as the convulsions diminished. She thought it had calmed down. It was dead.

She started again. The sink filled up with dead beasts. She tried steaming one. It changed colour slowly. Suffered even more. And still ended up dying.

Eleven lobsters in the sink. Only one still alive. Angelina sat down. Head in her hands, the world a gloomy place. She was disappointed. Terribly disappointed. And cross, as well. Because nothing else could explain *the* Lobster. His magic could only have come from this. His colour proved it. He had survived boiling water. At the end of her tether, lust stimulated by the bay leaf aroma, Angelina decided that it was after all possible that Lobster's gifts belonged to his species as a whole.

She took off her panties. Sat on the table. Pulled up her skirt. Picked up the still-living lobster. Positioned it in front of her cunt. It didn't move. She shook it, rubbing the pincers against her clitoris.

"Come on my boy, I'm giving you the most precious part of myself. Wake up a little. Don't I turn you on?"

The pain wrenched a high-pitched wail from deep inside her. The lobster fell to the tiled floor with the small piece of severed flesh in its pincer. Angelina collapsed to the ground, hands between her legs. Spinning round, doubled over. Spreading the river of blood flowing from her cunt. The lobster's tail slapped! Splattered! Angelina spun round; the lobster's tail slapped! Splattered! Angelina fainted.

When she regained consciousness it was daylight. The lobster was watching her. She could see from his moving antennae that he wasn't dead. His shell and pincers were stained with clotted red blood. So were Angelina's pubis and belly. And her hands, stuck between her legs. She felt weak. The wound between her lips was agony. Her clitoris was shrivelling, in the lobster's pincer. She realised she would be deprived of the root of orgasm for the rest of her life. The tree could no longer hope to nourish itself. Its leaves would fade. Its branches would die. She had no strength left for anger. Not against her body, which had never understood the song of men. Not against men, who had perhaps never known how to sing to it. She moved. It hurt. What is more intimate than pain? And as for pain and intimacy combined . . .

The cooked lobsters in the sink smelled awful. Angelina pulled herself up. Her dress fell back over her legs. She stood up, leaning on the edge of the table. Took a first step. Another. Another. She could move.

In the bathroom mirror she looked at her face, covered in clotted blood. Rubbed it with hot water, to make herself look more presentable. Washed her hands, leaving her nails as they were, black. She rubbed the front of her blouse and skirt with the flat of her palm. In this state, only the Chinese would be able to help her. She hid her body in a coat.

Chinatown. Angelina went into the "Red Dragon". The restaurant was murky. A young boy sat at a table by a window, opposite a man. A game of Go between them. Neither turned round as Angelina staggered past, her bum pushed out and thighs apart. She climbed the stairs, her face contorted with pain. A door on the first floor landing opened onto another stairway. Under the stairs was a little door. It creaked. Angelina felt better with the first whiff of opium. Dark floorboards reflected the dim light coming through the windows. Men were smoking on low divans. Angelina nodded to the old man kneeling behind a low table. He got up. Took her into another room. With a bed. A footstool. A chest of drawers, red, with lots of small compartments. Inside, pots of medicinal herbs. Angelina lay down. She was shaking. Chen gently unbuttoned the coat, revealing her blouse and bloodstained skirt. Angelina inched it up with the tips of her fingers. Chen looked carefully, not touching. Picked up her wrist; took the pulse. Poured a measure of yellow powder into a bowl. Covered it with hot water. Stirred it. Wiped the ivory stick. Helped her drink.

When she woke up, Angelina recognised the second floor room. It was where Chen brought her when she came to smoke. She felt clean. They'd dressed her in a pair of black pyjamas. She lifted the eiderdown with her legs. It hardly hurt now. She pulled the pyjama bottoms down. She was shaved. Her pubis was swollen. She spread her lips apart with her fingers. Slowly peeled away a piece of cloth covered in sticky brown paste. Two black threads stuck out from the folds of sown up flesh. Angelina wept.

She put the cloth back. Folded her lips in. Pulled the pyjamas up, and the eiderdown right to her nose. The tears flowed. No sobbing. Just tears, more and more tears. Later, she pulled on the cord to ask for help. Mui arrived, with his smile. And a tray. Soup. Angelina drank it and went back to sleep.

She woke up to smoke.

Alfred turned his key in the lock. Twice. Angelina must have gone out. He pushed the door open. The smell of rotting fish forced him to hold his nose.

Alfred had been born in this house. He was used to always being greeted by the same fragrance as he came in: that intimate smell of home, a mixture of earthy breeze from the cellar and dry leather from the attic, seasoned depending on the day with polish or bleach, and accompanied morning, noon and night by aromas from the kitchen of Rose Mary the housekeeper.

The handkerchief over his nose stopped him retching but didn't diminish his sick feeling. His mind was flooded by images of the doorway into the Quai d'Anjou building. That smell of gas. As strong as what he was smelling today. The neighbours hurtling down the stairs. Shouting all sorts of things. Him going up. Feeling dizzy. His eyes hurting. Getting to the flat and managing to open one window, then another. Taking Angelina out first. Her little eleven year old body, limp and pale, but alive. Carrying her out onto the street. The neighbours standing there on the Pont Marie. Laying her down on the pavement. Entrusting her to them. Going back up: to save Madeleine. Breathing in the gas. The second flight of stairs so long. Then crawling to Madeleine on all fours. It's all right here in his body, the feeling of trying to snatch Madeleine, his wife, his love, from the heavy jaws of death. Collapsing, weeping, on her unmoving belly. Shaking it with his sobs.

Alfred dropped his hanky. Went in. Rushed to the windows, creating air currents. Congealed blood in the rough shape of a human on the kitchen floor tiles. Flies everywhere. Traces of blood leading up the stairs to his daughter's room.

"It stinks of rotten fish, but not of death."

"Amenorrhea," the doctor had said, when Angelina was old enough to have her period but the blood didn't come. Alfred lay down on his daughter's bed, the windows wide open. He'd had enough of all these nights waiting up for her. You don't learn to stop fearing for your child; you just learn not to show it.

After Madeleine's death, they came back to New York. Angelina spoke French with him. It was she who wanted to. Her father's accent had always made her laugh; it softened the blow of his tempers. He hadn't got angry for a long time now. Not since he met Jennifer.

A window on the ground floor slammed shut. Alfred went into his own bedroom. Put on his painting clothes. Rolled up his sleeves. An anchor was tattooed on his right arm.

Angelina was in the kitchen. Sitting down. She'd undone her coat. The shiny satin of the Chinese pyjamas showed through. Her face was pale. She was staring fixedly at the imprint of her body on the floor. The fetid smell was starting to give way to the fresh air.

Alfred pulled out a chair. Sat down facing her. Angelina stroked her father's cheek. A childhood gesture; she used to do it before he kissed her, to make sure he wasn't scratchy. Alfred noticed a bay leaf aroma in her palm. The same smell as the leaves that Angelina had always picked from the big bay tree in Deauville, to make her laurel wreaths. She used to dance, trying to seduce him. He didn't feel anything. Was he repressing it? Now, it was too late even to wonder – over all these years his heart had grown a shell against the confusion of feelings. All these years, day after day, he'd watched her becoming a woman; watched her body slowly evolve, until she was a mirror image of Madeleine; the same infinitely long legs, the figure, the allure of the woman he loved so much he had even agreed to be a father.

Angelina pulled back her hands. Stood up. The pain between her legs was bearable. The first thing she did was pick up the lobster on the ground. It was still alive. The congealed blood on its shell had turned brown. The clitoris too was wrapped in a clot of blood. She threw it – with the lobster – into the crate, which Alfred filled with the other stinking lobsters. The flies were going crazy. Holding it away from his body, Alfred carried the crate into the living room. Put it in the fireplace. Angelina crumpled up paper, lit a match. The flames provoked a final convulsion from the surviving lobster. The fire crackled. For a long while, father and daughter stood hypnotised by the crematory dance.

Back in the kitchen, Alfred picked up a bucket and a hard brush. Poured bleach into very hot water and scrubbed. The fumes stung his eyes, his throat and the skin of his cheeks. The acid smell started to overcome the stink. When he wrung it, the mop excreted a greyish-pink liquid: blood waste.

Angelina turned off the tap so her father could hear her.

"I'm going back to Paris."

Alfred emptied the bucket into the sink.

"On your own?"

"Yes, on my own."

Alfred held back from reminding her that she'd never lived alone.

"And will you know how to get opium, there?"

Angelina froze; stunned at how far she'd underestimated what her father saw. "I've got a contact," she replied, eyes fixed on the water gurgling and whirling into the U-bend.

"Where are you planning to go?"

"Quai d'Anjou."

"I'm coming with you."

The scattered corpses around and inside the wreck of the *Titanic* were floating in water that tasted of stock. All by himself, Lobster had flavoured the sea for a few nautical miles.

Hundreds of lobster clusters worked furiously at flesh toughened by the cold of the water. Lobster reigned alone over the corpse of the old woman who had eaten his mother. Lobster was respected. He was the only one of his kind to have returned from the dead. His journey was evident from his red colouring and his smell. Those who escaped the *Titanic* aquarium had testified how these things had accompanied the death of their unfortunate companions.

The females were so taken with his bay leaf smell that they weren't even interested in food.

They just luxuriated in the *court-bouillon* fragrance, in a state of continuous arousal. To start with the males were too preoccupied with stuffing themselves to take any notice of their advances. But once full, they remembered the steps of the nuptial dance. The females were too impatient, surrendering themselves before the end of the ceremony. There were about a hundred females left over. They turned towards Lobster, who was interested only in Angelina. Threw themselves at him. Sheer abundance revived a taste for his own kind. He took them one by one, in the swarm of copulating males and females. Carried away by the frenzy of the moment, the throng spread out like a thousand tiny sparks in the darkness of the ocean.

After orgasm they uncoupled and stretched out, head to tail, belly up, pincers splayed out. And thus they rose, blissfully, from the night towards the light. A constellation of blue lobsters, with the red of Lobster right in the middle.

The Newfoundlanders couldn't believe their eyes. First they thought it was a spate of waves, with the dawn light shining through the foam. A blue light,

45

cold as the air. But then they realised. They weren't dreaming. These really were lobsters, floating to the surface in a position they'd never seen them assume before. At first they were angry: it must be a mass poisoning. They'd been saying for years that one day the sea was going to furiously gobble up the New World. But on closer inspection, they saw these lobsters were alive.

Their boats were already surrounded by such an expanse of crustaceans that there was no counting them. And more were continually floating to the surface. So many that after a while their sheer mass quelled the jerky movement of the waves. Soon, the animals were jammed up against each other. Clickety-clacking as their shells made contact. The fishermen didn't know what to think: miracle catch, natural disaster, attempted mass suicide . . . ?

Coming into contact with the air caused no change in the lobsters' behaviour. They wanted to stay with the experience they had just been through, even if it meant dying.

The three fishing boats formed a triangle. In the centre, bang in the middle of all the blue

shells, appeared Lobster. At that point the fishermen started praying. They saw in his redness the
eye of the Devil, cursing them. But then supersti-
tion was confronted by yet another, even more
troubling mystery; the aroma of bay leaves, drifting across the open sea, stronger even than the cod
piled in the hold.

Jules, the stoker, appeared on deck. He was
shouting, "We're in the Devil's Cauldron! He's
going to cook us!"

Before the others had time to react, he'd
thrown himself overboard. He didn't touch the
water, held aloft on the bed of lobsters. A carpet of
prickly feet. Jules was squirming like a worm.
Laughing. Trying to sit up, rolling and wriggling
about. Cracking up laughing. It was infectious,
soon they were all laughing. They'd never seen
such a scene. A buzz of laughter and clicking
lobster shells rose in an aromatic bay-leaf cloud
towards the limpid sky. From above, it looked like
a calm blue eye shadowed by foamy waves, in the
middle of the ocean.

Lobster, woken by the racket, couldn't understand why the men were laughing; didn't they

realise the danger Jules was in? He was only floating like that because the lobsters were languishing
in post-coital torpor. The fishermen leaning on
the bulwark were laughing harder and harder. But
Jules wasn't joking. The tickling was driving him
insane. Between each laughing fit he screamed,
"The Devil! The Devil!"

He rolled and slid towards Lobster, wanting to
pull his tail to ward off ill fortune, needing an end
to the torture, which he knew came from the Devil
in this disguise.

"The red gives you away!" he screamed once
more, before bursting out laughing, wriggling
about, inching, crawling right up to Lobster, who
grabbed one of his fingers and nipped it.

Overwhelmed by pain, Jules became quiet, still.
Lying on his back, he looked around. The fishermen had stopped laughing. They were looking at
their ocean brother, silent amid the clickety-clack
of the shells. They felt bad for letting down one of
their kind, for abandoning themselves to the
euphoria of fear. Jules told the Devil to go to hell!
Standing up on the lobsters, he ran, encouraged
by his brothers who threw him a length of rope.

Nantucket harbour was overrun by crowds. The three Newfoundland boats had collected a mountain of lobsters in their nets. The boats pitched as their loads scampered across the decks. Lobster shells crackled and crunched. This racket, already audible two nautical miles away, was louder even than the noise made by the men crowded onto the sea walls. No story had ever prophesied this.

The wind was suffused with the bay leaf aroma emanating from the females, perfumed since their contact with Lobster. After the initial euphoria, people started to worry.

"This is unnatural. Abundance today – but what about tomorrow?"

Their minds turned to the plagues of Egypt. A woman claimed she'd dreamt it.

"Smell! Smell! Can you smell it? It's bay leaves. Laurel means luck!"

"Too many lobsters kills the lobster," grumbled a merchant.

"No," cried his colleague, shouting to make himself heard over the hubbub of voices, shrieks, and clickety-clacks, "it's up to us to make something of it! Make them exceptional. The miracle catch. We can promote the Christ-like aspect of "the miracle lobsters": if we manage to get that across, they'll fetch four times the normal price."

A decision was taken about how to contain the enormous catch: block off the harbour dock, creating a huge fishpond. The three boats got to work. Fitted a net. Poured out the lobsters. Amid the silence of the crowd, the swarming of the lobsters crumpled the air like paper.

The fishermen had hardly stepped ashore before they began their impassioned speeches, each in his own way telling an unbelievable story. Groups formed around them. What they per-ceived as a miracle was so astounding it awoke corresponding vocabulary, gestures and inton-ations; they became storytellers of mountains and miracles. They were all talking about Jules. Jules saved from the sea; walking on the water; kissing the beast's forehead. The red lobster, which stretched their imagination beyond what could be imagined. The crowd demanded to see, if they were to believe in this living lobster wearing the cloak of death.

In the hold of the *Marie-Jeanne*, Jules was looking at Lobster. He was swimming in a barrel, full to the brim with seawater. Jules pulled up his jersey. Looked at his wounds, his flesh pierced by lobster feet. Purple marks all over his tattoos. He dipped his mangled finger into the water. Whispered.

"And to think that I took you for the Devil. The Devil wouldn't have saved my life. You're a messenger. A portent of life. You saw! The blue of my blood running over me. Like a Fauvist painting. Your mates tattooed me. We're brothers now. Blood brothers."

Despite the noise of the crowd Jules could hear footsteps on deck, and the voice of the *Marie-Jeanne* skipper, John, making a speech about this extraordinary day. About abundance. About the decision the three skippers had taken to give half the profits to the fund for fishermen's widows. There was clapping.

Jules could see into people's hearts. In the same way that he knew their skin. He had tattooed the whole crew. With his needle he could depict a tiger, Christ on the cross, a sailing ship in a tempest: he could make a precise copy of any image, but he couldn't write. His writing was illegible. Spelling was a word he didn't understand. He'd developed the deftness of his hands through locksmithing. He was an itinerant apprentice, but didn't complete his Tour de France – curiosity had led him to pick safes, much as he opened books: to learn some random part of life's great mystery. Because he could read. Slowly, but he could. In prison, he didn't study.

At night he dreamt of fishing, of the naked ocean. During the day he tattooed himself. His life in images. Then he did other people, in his own way becoming their scribe. Two of the bars of his cell were slightly bent, from his cell-mate's skull. He'd made advances to Jules. He died straight away. It took three guards to get him unstuck despite his small head. Jules told them that he'd thought he was a bird; that he'd wanted to fly away.

Jules recognised the voice of Mr Fu on deck. A Chinese merchant John traded with. He was talking about Lobster. Jules knew that there was an ancient tradition, in Chinese pharmacopoeia, of reducing bones, tusks and claws to powder and using them to make all kinds of elixirs for the revival of lazy male parts. To this lobster's advantage, his value lay in being alive. Jules could well imagine Mr Fu helping people to recover their virility by eating his droppings, touching his shell, drinking his aquarium water, inhaling the bay leaf aroma and even, why not, getting their pricks nipped by his pincers.

"At that price, you'll have to tell me what kind of water managed to cook him without killing him," Mr Fu was replying as he came into the hold with John.

"Well here we are – that's the one who jumped overboard," John said to Mr Fu, pointing at Jules asleep on the nets.

He walked up to the barrel. Took off the lid. Couldn't see Lobster. Stuck his arm in. Felt around the bottom, the sides, didn't find anything. Mr Fu noticed his concern.

"Is there a problem?"

John rushed at Jules. Shook him. The

53

tenderness of his injuries made Jules shove him away. John almost fell over. Went to hit Jules, who dodged, and held himself back from punching. John calmed down. He knew that Jules hit hard.

Jules, pretending to have just woken up, reminded John that the lobster's feet had left their mark. John apologised. Wanted to know where Lobster was. He wasn't in the barrel.

"I told you it was the Devil. It's better that he's gone. What kind of deal might he have offered? Something irresistible, I'm sure."

John didn't give a fuck about the Devil. He only believed in money. And this red lobster, back from the dead, could be worth a lot.

"He can't have climbed the ladder. He must be here somewhere." John became frantic. Mr Fu, unruffled, watched him running around, upending everything, finding nothing but fetid dirt. As he knocked everything over, John cursed the 'Redskins' he had fought during his youth, the way they disappeared when only a foot away. "This lobster must be from the same tribe."

Fuming with rage, he stopped with his hands clenched around Lobster's barrel. About to send it flying. Jules covered John's hands with his own and managed to calm him down. "Right now, this water is all we have left of him. It smells of him; it must share his powers."

John was quick to understand where his interests lay. Mr Fu came to take a sniff; tasted the water. He was suspicious that Jules and John were in league with each other. John, preoccupied with notions of price, thought it was a done deal; Jules had got a better sense of the Chinese merchant. He took off his jersey. Turned his back. Mr Fu looked at his injured body. Proof that what was being said on shore was in fact true. Mr Fu didn't want to miss a deal either. The miracle catch alone justified the value of the water in the barrel.

John dipped his hand in Lobster's water:

"Well, it's not helping me find this lobster – he hasn't been stolen for God's sake?"

"No," Jules replied, "but he might have flown away: perhaps he had feathers on his pincers, like the Redskins."

Mr Fu didn't believe in the Devil, but he had his own demons. A slow smile showed that his face wasn't a mask. John shut the barrel: against evaporation. He and Mr Fu went back on deck to negotiate.

Jules tipped up the barrel with one hand, sliding the other underneath; into a space just big enough to conceal his friend. He picked him up by the head. Looked into his eyes.

"They'll go out drinking tonight. The whole port will be drunk, and then we'll leave."

The cask was small. The size of a bucket. It didn't hold much water, but enough for Lobster to survive. The lid was closed. He didn't care about the lack of light. He could see in the dark. In any case he was being shaken around too much to be able to focus on anything properly. He felt almost nostalgic for the slatted crate that had carried him aboard the *Titanic*. Although it had been stifling, he'd been able to smell the earth.

Time went by. The bay leaf smell permeated the water, bringing back memories of Angelina. Her skin, almost as if he could touch it. He missed her so much it was killing him. Sweating an aroma that stimulated images, more images, all kinds of images, flooding his mind, suffocating him, confronting him with the pain of separation, the impossibility of touching her, of once again trailing his pincers through her pubic hair: it was awful. And the more he tried to stop himself from thinking, the more his body exuded this memory-inducing smell. Like sap! The water was turning into bay leaf juice. And the bumpier the road became, the sicker he felt. So soaked in humanness that in the end he threw up. The spasms were so violent that he banged his head; stunned, he fainted.

Lobster regained consciousness, his pincers trailing in the surf. Jules was holding him by the tail; dipping him in the waves; on a beach.

He was talking to him tenderly. Asking his forgiveness – since they'd left he'd been preoccupied with unforeseen events. From now on he would take the ocean route all the way to New York. So he could change Lobster's water every day.

The cold waves make Lobster's shell tingle, signalling his forthcoming moult. That specific shellfish trait hadn't even crossed his mind. His human condition had made him forget. Shedding his shell! That would mean shedding Angelina. What an awful thought. Lobster doesn't want this moult. It's all very well for shellfish. He persuades himself that he's different: he may be feeling the first signs of moulting, but it's just a leftover from his previous species, fossilised in the red of his shell. From now on he belongs to a new race, the *Red Lobster* race.

Tonight, sucking-pig cooked on a spit. As it was cooking, Lobster thought he recognised a smell in the smoke. It was when the morsel Jules fed him reached his mandibles that he realised what it was. It tasted like the old woman who had eaten his mother. With every mouthful, images of the *Titanic* came flooding back: the ring of corpses; Angelina, up close.

Jules wiped his mouth. Picked Lobster up by the head. Went to rinse him in the waves. Noticed the flabbiness of the shell. He knew what it meant. He'd handled lobsters for eighteen months. He used to throw the flabby ones back into the sea: you couldn't sell them.

He ran his fingers all over Lobster as he plunged him into the water. Lobster was ticklish through the softened shell. He wriggled with laughter. Didn't know what it was. He remembered Jules giggling hysterically on the carpet of lobsters; their pointy feet tickling him as his fingers were doing now. He understood. And he laughed. From the tickling as much as the discovery of laughter. He tried to think of Angelina's supple skin. How he could make her laugh. But Jules's fingers were driving him crazy. Crazy from laughing. He struggled. Jules thought he was trying to escape. Held him more firmly. Lobster couldn't breathe. He stopped laughing. Jules slackened his grip. Put him on the sand to get his breath back. Changed the water in the cask.

In the faint light of the embers, Jules pulled a piece of paper from his breast pocket; it had been there for months: the agreement between him and Marcel. Their version of a bill of sale. A written guarantee. Jojo, the waiter at the Café de la Rotonde, had written it. His handwriting was beautiful.

It said that Marcel promised to sell his tattoo parlour to Jules. The agreement was valid for two years. Jules had two months to get to Paris.

"Don't worry, my friend," he told Lobster, "we'll get there in time. In New York I'm going to find us a ship bound for France."

The ocean had not yet calmed after the storm; the waves were still rough. Angelina pushed her hair back against the evening wind, on the deck of the ocean liner *Aquitaine*. No sleep for two days; the lack of opium; and yet something was holding her back, behind the rail. Two days of ocean fury during which Alfred had fought sleep; fought his foreboding; fought the fear that this sight of his daughter in the wind would be his last.

During these two days he had distinctly seen Angelina's spirit flirting with the sea, calling her body to accompany it. He would stay here. Right here. Wouldn't sleep. Like after the incident. When he had come back down to the Pont Marie and she was no longer there. He found her at the Hôtel-Dieu hospital. Still unconscious. Stayed awake at her bedside. Talked to her. Waiting, not knowing. At night the shouts in the corridors helped him fight sleep. He wasn't going to leave her. After two days, she woke up.

Alfred had never underestimated the pull of her mother's country, but he had hoped that the ocean crossing would put her off. What scared him now was the realisation that, for Angelina, the sinking of the *Titanic* had been a missed opportunity.

"Let's go and eat, it'll do us good."

Angelina moved towards her dad. Snuggled into his shoulder so that her whole body was leaning towards him, facing the sea. Nestled her head in the hollow of his neck. Alfred slipped his hand under her elbow. And with his daughter thus positioned, made his way to the dining room. The sudden pitches of the ship sometimes affected the direction they took, but never knocked them off balance. The deserted gangways stank of vomit. Passengers were in their cabins, praying for the ocean to calm. There weren't enough sailors to clean the place up.

Only the captain, the first mate, and a few

passengers were in the dining room. Three musicians, so used to the pitching it had no effect on them, made the place seem like a dance hall deserted by the wedding party. Even the lights were nauseating.

Angelina wouldn't eat a meal in these conditions. She pulled away from her father. Alfred hesitated. Decided to let her go. In the end, what could he do in the face of his daughter's determination?

Angelina on the bridge. Handrail. Safety rail. Against the flow. Against the boat. Against the wind. Against life. Resist death. Down the stairs. Metal. Her footsteps ringing out. Passing some crew. Seeing vague silhouettes bent over in the night, throats burning with bile. The raging sea. Down from deck to deck. Looking for whatever might hold her back. The call so strong. Down lower. Nearer the water. Impossible, so near to her father; but death so near as well. Wanting to take refuge. Protect herself from the call of the deep.

The door was heavy. The wind burst in with

her. The burning of overheated air. Needing all her strength to shut the door behind her. Standing on the footbridge looking over the machine room. The open boilers. Men stoking them. Constantly, in this excessive heat, feeding the insatiable appetite of a ten-mouthed beast. Their bodies gleamed red in the light of the flames. Imps under a sky of iron and steel. Angelina undid her coat. Put it on the guardrail. Unbuttoned the collar of her blouse. Under her velvet dress she was streaming. She wanted to leave. But the icy wind would whistle through her clothes soaked in sweat; she knew it might kill her. And she didn't want that kind of death.

Jules was stoking boiler number six. It was blazing. He never would have thought his rough fisherman's hands would blister. He shut the firebox with the end of his shovel. Pressed his thumb and forefinger together; to feel Lobster's scar; to give himself a boost. Three of the stokers had been off sick since the storm. His legs were heavy. His exhausted eyes no longer even tried to see properly, content with making out shapes. With a tap of his shovel he undid the latch of boiler number seven, at the foot of the stairs. Opened it. More flames. Fire. Black coal.

Angelina descended the stairs. Her dress and petticoats clung to her skin, hindering her movements. Down. Sweat in her eyes. Dusty tears. Salty lips. Down. Afraid, almost. Of her feelings? No, of the heat. She wasn't used to it. It was almost 60° centigrade. And there was coal dust everywhere. At the foot of the stairs, face to face with Jules. Stripped to the waist. His sweat: bay leaves.

Angelina trembled. Her cunt wanted to weep, but it was her eyes that cried. The more they cried the more she froze. She became a rock, not a woman. Jules was helpless. How should he approach her? And him so tired. He put a hand on her shoulder. Felt her pain through the damp cloth. Couldn't understand how beauty could suffer this much. Despite her blinding tears Angelina was able to make out his tattoos. He put on his shirt; sky blue; it went black as soon as it touched his soaking skin. She wanted to know more. At least his name. She gave him hers. What did these tattoos mean? She wanted to know. Insisted.

The women he had known had never listened to him. And he hadn't wanted to hear their stories. So what about this woman? She wasn't his kind. Out of his class. Rich. But he trusted her. She came from the same family of pain. It was her skin! The little he could see of it was enough. This woman made him feel in his skin. Their flesh was in harmony. He started to talk. To tell. Because he'd been abandoned, he'd invented his own date of birth. The first of January. He told. The big landmarks of his life. His meeting with Marcel the tattoo artist. Learning the profession. The Paris tattoo studio he was going to buy from Marcel. He opened up. Usually so stilted with words, unable to write, he was able to say the kind of things you only write in a diary.

Angelina listened to his words; her sexual response was nil. She looked away. Her hands flailed in the emptiness, awkward. She had to leave. Jules's momentum was cut short. He felt ridiculous. Humiliated. Crippled. His mouth full of words he never should have said. Anger moved through his fists to reach his eyes.

He whispered, "Go through the kitchens

and you'll get to the upper deck without stepping outside. It's easy."

Angelina went. Without a word of apology. She didn't want to apologise; wanted to make herself hated for what she was; definitively.

Jules looked at his hands. Compass roses tattooed on his palms, under the black of the coal. He'd endured the pain by muttering to himself that they would "make storms rage in women's breasts". The ship was no longer pitching. The storm had calmed. Jules walked along the gangways. It was his mind that was pitching. "I should have kissed her. What came over me, talking to her?"

He pulled the cask out from under his bunk. Lifted the lid. Lobster had lost his moulted shell. Pale red, it was floating in the water. His new shell had formed. It was blue, like any Brittany lobster. Jules had known that this day would come. It didn't change anything. They had become brothers the day they met. This was his friend. His saviour. The one who had understood his laugh: the death lurking behind it.

Jules picked up the shell. It was as big as his

hand. Felt it for the last time. Swore loyalty to Lobster. Opened the porthole and put his hand out. The moon was high. The ocean smooth, fringing the ship's stem; a foamy lip. Jules looked at the dead skin quivering in the wind. He wasn't sure when solitude had singled him out. He'd always held himself apart; in the shade, so he could see the glimmer of his internal world. He let go of the shell. The bay leaf aroma became weaker. The red returned to the ocean; swirled; was carried away by the current.

Jules carried the cask along a dark, rusty corridor to the hold. Put it down. Stuck his hand in. Slipped it under Lobster's belly. It was pliant. Lobster had got used to Jules's fingers. They no longer tickled him. He didn't want to laugh at all. Jules pulled him out of the water. His shell was soft. Vulnerable. His pincers and tail hung down. Jules sniffed at him. He smelled of iodine; no hint of bay leaf. He put him on the ground. Turned on the saltwater tap. Collected water in his cupped hands and poured it gently.

Lobster wanted to die. Unrecognisable to Angelina, his perfume evaporated – what reason was there to live? Living among humans had been a strategy for finding her again.

Go back to being a lobster?! After all he had been through, even if Jules were to put him back in the water the very thought of rocks, seaweed, and the murkiness of the depths filled him with horror. He had tasted the light of human living and he could no longer do without it.

His feelers pointed forward, searching out Jules's palms. Found them. Snuggled up against them. They had a different smell. Something other than the usual smell of fire. There was a bitterness in the coal dust. An emotion. Lobster looked at Jules. His eyes! A fever was veiling his brotherly gaze. Lobster explored the warmth of his hands, perceived yet another smell. A hint of salt diluted in amber. Perfumed sweat. A woman's sweat amid Jules's. The sweat of the only woman he knew. The only woman he loved. Angelina!

Jealous. He yanked his feelers back. His pincers opened and closed. He fumed at their flabbiness. His mandibles got all worked up. His spittle was boiling. Bubbles of spit flowed from his mandibles, one after another. But he couldn't say anything Jules could understand. What suffering – this inexpressible jealousy, this human consciousness deprived of language, but not of thought. It was she who calmed him. Prompted him to think: Jules, in love with Angelina! His unexpected chance to see her again. But his shell was blue. And he no longer smelled of bay leaves. Never mind: he was still Lobster. The one who had returned from the dead. He began to believe in destiny.

The carriage was noisy. Angelina looked out of the window, hands huddled in the pockets of her shipwreck coat. Alfred had been staring at her since they left Le Havre. At certain moments she looked unrecognisable: overwhelmed by the fear of returning to her childhood city, to the little one-bedroom flat her mother refused to leave, even after Angelina was born. Awful scenes played in her mind. But she wouldn't give up. She had to return; she had to see; so that she could leave.

In the shadowy light Alfred noticed how much she looked like Madeleine, and Madeleine's father. Only the eyes were his. And the obsessive hand-sniffing was new.

Paris was steeped in winter. As they neared the Seine, Angelina felt reassured. Since the shipwreck any deep water had become a promised sea; a reunion with Lobster; even though they all hid blood and guts beneath the shimmering surface.

When the cab stopped at the Quai d'Anjou and Angelina stepped onto the pavement where ten years earlier her father had laid her, unconscious, she realised that whole story belonged to a different time. In these stony surroundings only the river seemed alive. The front door was just a door among many others. The hall smelled the same as ever. The concierge looked at them from behind a drawn curtain, just as she had always done.

When she saw Angelina, there wasn't a moment's doubt. She was the spitting image of Mme Benheim, who she'd never been able to bring herself to call by her married name.

Because of all this, she didn't come out of her lodge. For her, this was the past coming back. She'd never thought she'd see them again. Seeing Alfred's body silhouetted in the doorway, she wasn't sorry for the things she'd said. Her questions about the gas leak. Why save your daughter first?

Angelina noticed her cold eyes. The curtain didn't close. Those eyes were following her, just as they had always done when she was a child.

The new carpet on the stairs didn't hush the memory of her first high-heeled shoes. And even though Angelina felt that with every step she climbed she was passing through the little girl tearing down the stairs towards the embankment, it didn't change her conviction that all this was dead. She dug her hand into her pocket; pulled it straight out again. Smelled her fingers. On reaching their landing, Alfred gave her the keys so she could open.

Everything was there. In its right place. As she remembered. Alfred had made sure it was looked after all these years. Everything was familiar to Angelina. She could locate everything. Except the sense of tragedy. It was simply an apartment she'd lived in with her mum and dad. Where she fainted. Where her mother died. She didn't feel like she belonged here any more. All that was happening was that she remembered the place. No emotion. Her past was past.

Rue de la Roquette. Night, crystallising the cold. La Rotonde closed. No sign even of Jojo sleeping. The immortal Jojo. Long bony arm in a white shirt, bent into a V-shape under a heavy tray. Twelve hours a day without complaint. He must have been born doing it. Waiter. More than a vocation; it was an identity.

Further along, on the opposite pavement, was the tattoo parlour. Jules had been away for two years, and it was exactly the same. The crunching underfoot as he walked up to the door. The familiar noise of coal splintering under his feet. It was light enough that he could see a black cloud of it on the pavement. He put Lobster's cask down. Opened the bag slung across his shoulder. Got what he needed to sort the lock. His hands were frozen; he rubbed them to get the movement back. Lobster was moving about restlessly. Pushing up the lid with his pincers. Poking his feelers out. Splashing. Jules had never seen him so jittery.

"What's up? Can't wait to get in?"

Jules pushed the picklock in. His thawed hands managed to get a sense of the mechanism; it gave.

When they went in it smelled of death. Lobster was going crazy. Jules pushed him down to the bottom of the cask. Weighted the lid with his bag. He could hear him bashing against the wood.

The studio was a mess. There'd been a fight. But all the talismans were still there – the tiger's head, the boxing glove. But not the anchor. The one from Marcel's father's barge.

Dried blood on the floor. Surrounded by faint black footprints.

Jules wasn't surprised. Good old Marcel! He always was a feisty one. Kicking up a fuss. Taking people for idiots. It had to happen: the coal barrow; the body dumped on it; straight to the Seine.

"Black star nights," as they were known in the area. Because of the coal that sank with the corpse.

Jules hugged the slip of paper to his chest. Now he could keep all that money. Clean money. Earned from eighteen months' worth of fishing, stinking of cod. Marcel was dead; gone, in the eyes of the law; unless he floated back up to the surface. So long as no one arrived to claim the studio, all he had to do was move in. Find an aquarium for Lobster. The cask was shaking from his blows. Jules took the bag off. Picked up the lid. Lobster appeared, like a devil. Scrambled up. Tumbled out of the cask. Straight to the pool of dried blood. Two hours later the floor was clean. The scene of a crime was a shop once more.

Winter had become total with nightfall. The Parisians walked fast. Necks sunken. Fists tight in pockets. Bodies turned inwards against the cold. Bereft of the alluring, proud, slightly contemptuous gaze of spring. The Seine was in full spate, the moon reflected on its surface.

Angelina crossed the Pont Marie, a passenger on a stone ship. An elegant figure. The sound of her footsteps. The steam of her breath. She turned around. Looked back towards the apartment. Her father had left the light on. He always left a light on for her. With this cold he would have laid out a pair of flannel pyjamas on the thick eiderdown of her bed.

When she gets back, after he's gone to bed, it's always the same. He pretends he wasn't sleeping.

With a book in his hand, as proof. But he always forgets to put his glasses on.

She won't even have taken her coat off and he'll already have milk on the stove. His remedy. For as long as she can remember he's made her hot milk to help her sleep. His very best maternal gesture. And they can't avoid each other in this apartment. Not like in New York. Here the ceilings are disproportionately high. There's only one bedroom. Angelina sleeps in the living-dining room; she insisted. Alfred tried everything – that ever since she was born he and Madeleine had slept there, even that she was treating him like an old man. She didn't give in.

Living in such a small, crowded space sometimes made Angelina revert to childhood habits. How she brushed her hair, or the way she lifted her heels right up as she walked. Numerous little signs that she was quite aware of, but knew came from a bygone time.

They'd been here a month. She'd gone out to smoke three times – the only nights she hadn't come home, unable to face her father's gaze. At those times she was so aware of the pain he hid behind the softness in his eyes. So, on opium days, she came home in the afternoon. Once the traces had gone. She got her complexion from her mother: outrageously fresh.

On the Quai des Celestins, two men in top hats slowed to watch her pass. They didn't know what to make of this elegant woman heading towards the Bastille.

When she got there, she came across some pimps. She wasn't afraid. She lived with death beckoning her; she had nothing to lose, which created a distance between her and the crooks, ruffians and other nasties milling around those parts of town. They could whistle, they could brush past; they didn't know how to provoke her. She was disconcerting. Her beauty as well as her determination. An unknown species. Aloof from the riff-raff, the sweating masses.

She turned into the rue de la Roquette. She used to walk down here with her mother as a little girl. Going to put flowers on her grandmother's grave at Père Lachaise. Every Sunday, if it was sunny. Angelina used to love losing herself in the myriad paths, reading people's names on the graves. One Sunday, passing by two marble tombstones, she saw her grandmother's surname inscribed on one of them. There was a star, not a cross. Her mother explained: though her grandmother was a Catholic, she had a Jewish name.

Jules was sitting in La Rotonde, on the corner of rue de la Roquette and rue Saint-Sabin, smoking brown tobacco. He occupied his usual spot, in front of a mirrored pillar. He could see the shop-front in its reflection. Angelina was standing in front of the shop door.

He hadn't tried to find her again on the *Aquitaine*, but he'd felt her presence in him for the whole journey. He watched her disembark at Le Havre, with a man he would have taken for her husband if he hadn't overheard her calling him 'dad'. He'd never said that word. Or 'mum'. Angelina hadn't looked back – not even with that reflex most people have: one last look at what you're leaving behind.

Standing on the deck of the *Aquitaine*, Jules felt his blood turn to stone. He couldn't even wave. "Is this love?" How he wished that he had a friend he could ask. For a long time after she disappeared, he stood there gazing at the crowd.

With her hands cupping her eyes, and her nose against the glass pane in the door, trying to see into the darkness of the shop, Angelina didn't hear him coming. She jumped when he moved her aside to get to the lock.

He didn't say anything. Put the key in. Opened the door. Ushered her in. Angelina understood his silence. Did nothing to break it.

The shop was long and narrow. Two red velvet benches on either side. The walls lined with tattoo designs, grouped according to subject. Jules had Angelina sit down. Went behind the counter that blocked off the end of the room. Walked down a narrow corridor to the kitchen. Refilled the wood-burning stove. A big pot of tepid water was on top of it. Vegetables nearby, chopped and ready to cook. Above, on a shelf, Lobster in his aquarium. You could hardly see him behind the steamed-up glass. Jules wiped the glass clean with the back of his hand. Dipped his finger into the water. Lobster didn't reply.

Angelina was still wearing her coat. She watched Jules come back with a bottle of gentian. He poured out two glasses. She stood up to take the one he held out to her. Jules took a gulp that he kept in his mouth for a long while; she hardly touched hers.

After swallowing he asked, "So you want a tattoo?"

"Yes. I've looked at the designs on the walls, but you don't have what I want."

"And what do you want?"

"A lobster."

Jules believed in synchronicity. But he couldn't begin to imagine the bond between Lobster and Angelina. Lobster was sure he recognised Angelina's voice from his aquarium. He raised his feelers out of the water. But he couldn't hear very well from the kitchen.

"A Brittany lobster?" Jules asked.

"Red, if possible," replied Angelina.

"Cooked?"

"Um," she hesitated, "yeah, if you like, cooked."

"It's not a question of liking it – a red lobster is a cooked lobster."

"In that case I want a cooked lobster."

"And where do you want it?"

"Below my belly button."

"Below the navel or on the pubis?"

"Below the navel, above the pubis."

"Is this your first one?"

"Yes."

"You know it hurts. There, at least."

"It doesn't matter."

Jules finished his drink. Closed the curtains of the window onto the street. Dragged one of the benches into the middle of the room.

"You can lie down."

Angelina undid her coat. Lay down. Unbuttoned the front of her dress. Pulled up the bottom of her blouse. Her skin was bare from the navel to the pubis. Her panties were satin. Edged with lace. She had her arms crossed under her breasts. Her body was fragrant. The small expanse of exposed flesh gave off a musky aroma of hawthorn.

"All right? Not cold?"

"No, not at all."

Jules sat on a stool by Angelina's belly. Pulled up a small table laden with needles and inks. Used his penknife to sharpen a thick pencil. Pulled the skin tight with his left hand.

"Do you want the pincers pointing upwards or downwards?"

"Downwards."

He outlined the lobster's shape with a few strokes of his pencil.

"Have a look and tell me if it's OK."

Angelina sat up.

"That's perfect."

Jules smeared vaseline over the drawing. The thin, black outline of the lobster looked almost like a keyhole. Jules dipped his needle into the red ink. Stretched the skin taut. Leaned a little closer and injected. His movements were quick. The marks from the needle followed the pencil outline. Blood formed. He wiped it away. The belly tensed instinctively.

"Are you all right?"

"It stings," replied Angelina.

Jules got back to work. Angelina didn't say a word. She sweated. From heat. From emotion. And her fragrance spread.

In the kitchen, Lobster pricked up his

antennae. He could smell her. "It's her! It's her!" he cried to himself. Tossed about. Lashed out with his tail. Water overflowed from the aquarium. Evaporated on the wood stove. He'd always known they were meant for each other.

Angelina was starting to become aware of Jules's smell. His spicy sweat. And his hands on her belly. Hot. The blood that he wiped away. Her stained panties. Belly button rising and falling. Opening and closing along with her breath. Controlling the pain.

The water in the pot starts to boil. The steam mists everything up. Escapes from the kitchen. Gently envelopes Angelina and Jules. Becomes impregnated with their fused aromas.

Lobster is overcome by jealousy. He wishes he could laugh at it. Pinches his own belly. Too rigid. His jealousy is everywhere. Even though he knows that human males can't please her. That he's the only one in the world who can love and satisfy her. That she's his, because he saved her from drowning; from freezing. Just as he saved Jules, who is right now betraying him.

86

Lobster can't understand any more. Whose instrument is he? They rescued each other, yet now his shell is burning with jealousy for this man who says he's his brother, this man he can sense bent over the body of his beloved in the next room; his Angelina who is giving off the same aroma as she did on the staircase. So Jules must be able to love her.

He remembers Jules throwing his moult out of the porthole.

He hauls himself up. By his pincers. Balances on the edge of the aquarium. Lets himself fall into the boiling water.

Jules put down his needle. The blood on the small tattooed lobster was blending with the red of the ink. Jules wiped. Spread vaseline. Wiped again. More vaseline. Angelina grabbed his hand. Jules let her. Holding his palm against her skin, she slid it under her panties; right to her vulva.

"It's wet, but dead. Don't hate me."

Jules's fingers stayed still.

"I'm angry with you, but not for that."

87

He pulled his hand away. Got to his feet in the humid room. Angelina didn't move. He went to the kitchen. It was completely steamed up. Took two cloths and removed the pot of boiling water from the stove. Covered it.

When he came back, Angelina was still lying down. Shivering.

"What's up?" he asked her.

"I must have caught a chill on my way here."

"Don't you want to see?"

"Of course."

Jules helped her sit up. She put her hands either side of the tattoo. Looked at it carefully.

"It's exactly as I'd imagined."

Jules put a compress on it. Angelina held it in place with her finger. He wrapped a bandage several times around her waist, fastening it with a safety pin.

Angelina buttoned herself up. Drank her glass of gentian. Asked for another. Stood up. Put on her coat. Paid Jules.

"I'll see you home," he said.

"I'm fine. I can walk."

"Maybe, but at this time of night it's better I come with you."

Jules took her hand. It was hot. Very hot. She didn't pull away. Quite the opposite. Held his hand tight. Jules felt proud walking down the street hand in hand. As if her beauty made him handsome. Angelina let him lead the way. He enjoyed the steam rising from their breath. The way it blended in front of them. Angelina focused on that so as not to faint. Not to let the ache in her bones take over. The cold was dry. The night was dark. She noticed how handsome Jules was.

"We're here," she said, pointing to the lit window of her apartment.

Jules smiled at her. He'd tattooed her. Marked her. An indelible bond would always link them. Angelina turned. Pushed open the front door.

In the stairway, Angelina started shivering. Struggled to get up the stairs. Dropped her key on the landing. Picked it up. Turned it smoothly in the lock. Went in. Closed the door, taking care to release the knob gently. Huddled up to the stove. So close it almost burned. But it didn't warm her.

She waited for her father to enter the room. He didn't.

On the bookshelf sat a bulging file: "Titanic". Full of press cuttings, survivors' testimonies, their diverse feelings about having survived.

Angelina read the names again and again. She couldn't stop.

Guilt? If she had truly loved life, would she have felt guilt? She'd so often been envious of that emotion! At least it would mean she was alive; alive in this world that made everyone guilty.

She shut the file. She would end her life by drowning. To put things back in order. Die as she should have died. If Lobster hadn't opened the doors to orgasm, she never would have taken the lifeboat. She would have smoked opium. Then sung with the men, glass in hand. It would have been the perfect time to take the plunge. Suicide disguised as shipwreck would have spared her father the pain of a child dying from disgust at life; at the world; at other people. She wouldn't have needed that place next to the grey woman; how many people had died still wanting to live?

Die now. It was the perfect season. The Seine

was so cold it would freeze her muscles and cut off her breathing. She would be sure to sink straight to the bottom; she didn't know how to swim.

She took off her coat and lay down fully dressed. Shivering. Her groans woke Alfred; he came to her bedside. Tucked her in. Felt her forehead. Pushed back her hair. Her face, thus revealed, was freakishly similar to her mother's. Her skin was shining with sweat. The greyish-ultramarine eyes had lost their sparkle.

Alfred kept thinking about the little girl she used to be. He couldn't bear the sound of her teeth chattering, and her confused murmurings, saying she didn't want to "die like this".

He pushed the sofa up to the stove. Peeled back the covers. The sheets. Undid the buttons of her dress. His fingers, made clumsy by his daughter's trembling, continued to the bottom. He loosened the laces of her boots. Pulled them off. Sat on the couch and slipped a hand under her back to lift her up. The density of her body surprised him. He pulled her towards him to get the dress off her shoulders. Her nipples, beneath the sodden blouse, left two round imprints on his pyjama top. Angelina couldn't hold her head up; she flopped against her father's neck. Once the top part of her dress was off, Alfred pushed his daughter back down, supporting her with his left arm. He could feel the roundness of her skull against his palm. Her drenched hair. He held her away from him. Undid her blouse. His fingers brushed her breasts; her belly; right down to the pubis.

He discovered the bandage circling her waist. Her bloodstained panties. He thought she'd been injured. Shook her, wanting to know.

"It's nothing daddy. Nothing. An image. A souvenir, daddy. Nothing serious."

He peeled the blouse away from the skin. Tugged the bandage aside to find out what it concealed. Angelina was shivering all over.

"A lobster? Why a lobster?" he whispered in Angelina's ear.

She didn't reply.

He tossed the blouse and dress to the foot of the bed. Pulled his daughter to him. Undid her bra. Angelina was burning up. Alfred stretched her out on the bed. Took hold of the shoulder straps and slid them down her arms. Angelina was rambling, babbling: the shipwreck, Maurice, Lobster, his pincers, orgasm, Jules.

Alfred took her tights off. Hesitated over the panties. Looked away as he pulled them down her legs.

The nearby stove heightened the stench of fever. She smelled of bay leaves. Alfred looked at his daughter's naked shivering body. His daughter had always left him a stranger to desire. She was burning up. Was this a final bid? A last cry for love? The sheet and mattress were soaked. He dried Angelina with towels. Slid his hands under her arms and legs and carried her into the bedroom. Put her into his bed, on Madeleine's side. Covered her with a sheet. Lay down beside her. Her heat, her trembling, her sweat poured through the material.

"My little girl." Those were the words that came to him as tears streamed down his cheeks. He pulled the covers over them both.

Back in his shop, Jules tidied away the inks and needles. Left the bench where it was. Poured another glass of gentian. Sank it in one.

In the kitchen, he fed the stove. Saw the vegetables chopped and ready for cooking. Remembered he was going to make soup. Put the still warm pot on the stove. Took off the lid. The water smelled of the sea. Lobster was floating there. Red. Dead.

When he saw his friend, he thought of Angelina's tattoo. Started to feel like a pawn in a story not of his own making. This woman, whom he felt he could love, wanting a lobster tattooed on her belly. His brother, preferring to be red and dead than alive and blue. He'd thrown himself into the pot.

Suicide. He couldn't have fallen in by accident. Perhaps Jules should have set him free? The idea hadn't even occurred to him. Yet he felt like a wildcat caged in the human jungle, and this animal had seemed just like him.

Jules picked Lobster up by the head and pulled him out of the pot. He was overcooked. According to Jules when you lost a friend, the greatest proof of love was to not lose your appetite. Carry on living. As long as the friendship had been affirmed daily, the disappearance of a brother should cause no regret. Regrets only come when you haven't lived. And with Lobster, Jules had lived intensely. He knew he would miss him. But today, the greatest proof of love would be to eat him.

He tossed Lobster onto the chopping board. Split him down the middle with a single stroke of the knife. Used the handle to break open his pincers. Flash-fried him in a red hot pan, shell side first, then belly.

A good white plate and his Lobster on it, smelling beautifully of lobster. A knob of butter, salt, pepper, knife and fork. Wine. Red.

Jules started with the tail. He'd eaten better in

Newfoundland. But they weren't his brother. Which gave this one a unique flavour. He took a drink between each mouthful. From time to time he examined the progression of stains on the big napkin tied round his neck; like you evaluate the development of a painting. It made him squint. He was a bit drunk.

It was a beautiful day, that particular beauty of winter sun. Crystal-clear light, so you can see for miles. Alfred looked out of the window at the sky reflected in the river. Angelina was sleeping. She was still feverish. As he looked at the Seine it was her pale and trembling body that he was thinking of.

He'd changed the sheets three times during the night. He kept remembering it all. The smells. Angelina's ramblings: the red shell she talked about at the peak of her fever. What did she mean? His old flannel pyjamas? He'd never had such soft, red ones. They were so old, Madeleine's last present before she died. There was still a scrap of them in the shoe-cleaning box. A scrap of shoe-shining cloth. He could remember the day he decided to stop sleeping in them. He'd held out for years, despite the unravelling seams that scratched his knees, elbows, and bottom. For years. And every morning Angelina would come into his bed. He remembered how he would turn to the side to deflect those full-frontal embraces. How naturally she would press up against him. He'd never succumbed to his baby's innocence.

Alfred was exhausted from his sleepless night. He stoked up the fire and lay down next to Angelina.

Jules woke bathed in sweat. He put it down to his dreams: he'd been swimming underwater. And he didn't know how to swim.

His bedroom, opposite the kitchen, looked over an internal courtyard. A small window let in greyish light. At this time in the morning, the stove had been out for hours. He was usually so sensitive to the cold; but he was giving off a huge amount of heat. Wellbeing. An inner warmth unfamiliar to him. With a sweep of his hand he uncovered his drenched body; the sheets and covers flew to the foot of the bed. The disturbed air gave off a smell of bay leaves. His mind sputtered with the memory of being pierced by thousands of tiny feet. He brought his forearm to his nose; he could smell that crazy moment. His hands! They too smelled of his brother. His whole body smelled like Lobster.

He wheeled round to stand up. Felt a stinging between his thighs. He put his hand there, and pulled it away instinctively. Sitting on the edge of the bed, he couldn't believe what he saw between his legs; despite the poor light, he could see it very well: his cock was covered with a lobster's shell. Red.

His first instinct was to try and pull it off. All that happened was a yelp of pain. His whole body was wracked with the spasms of Lobster being scalded. A mad, inexplicable vision passed before his eyes. He was swimming, underwater. It appeared that Lobster's red pincers had taken the place of his hands. Angelina was arched backwards, seemingly climaxing.

The images faded with the pain. Jules looked at his cock. He felt he understood. A present from his brother? To help him love Angelina? What he imagined next made him quiver.

The base of the shaft was free. He took hold of it there. He could move it in any direction, almost like before. His fingers brushed over the surface. It was hard, but as sensitive as his skin. He stood up. Took a few steps. Had to walk with his legs apart to avoid hurting himself. Went to the loo. He could still piss. It felt the same, but smelled different. That bay leaf smell.

The strangest part was handling something so rigid yet so sensitive. His fingers moved naturally up the shaft to empty the canal; got scratched on the sharp joints.

He went over to the counter. Picked up a bandage. Sat down on the bench still in the middle of the shop. Daylight shone through the yellow curtains. He bandaged his prick so that he could walk without resembling a monkey, and piss without cutting his fingers.

He did it meticulously. Wound the bandage in two diagonal layers. Left as much as possible open to the air.

He lay down on the bench. The velvet still smelled of Angelina. Mechanically, he started playing with himself. Primordial instinct. He felt energy radiating from his cock. It swelled. He undid the bandage. His prick was erect. The shell had softened. Become looser. Flexible. It had kept its fluted shape. But there was nothing that would cause hurt. "It really is a present," Jules exclaimed. The red had turned orange. His fingers started to work the shaft. All the sensations were still there. And new ones as well. That started in his groin and spread right to his feet. And his head. And hands. He grabbed hold of the penis with his whole hand. Started jerking off. The harder his cock became, the more the shell softened. Defences stepping aside for life. Angelina was everywhere. This cock would make her come. Jules was sure of it. He thanked Lobster. Lobster who'd chosen him to give this woman the pleasure essential to life. The bastard was here. He was going to come. He spurted! Arched his back. Hot sperm on his belly. Let himself go. Abandoned to a toe-curling climax.

Angelina opened her eyes. Alfred was asleep next to her. She was no longer feverish. Still in bed, she tucked the covers around her father. Then got up. Her tattoo was covered in little brown scabs. Like a real shell. She put on her warmest clothes. The shipwreck coat. Stoked the fire, sat down at her desk, and wrote.

Daddy,
I've often spotted you looking tearful. I used to think it was mum, until one day I realised it was because of me.
I love you.
Angelina

She stuck her hand unconsciously into her pocket. Sniffed the back of her fingers.

She opened the door. Pulled her key out quietly. The lock was silent.

When she got to the Pont Marie, she felt a craving for opium; the desire to escape rather than die. She pushed away the craving, the habit.

Angelina hitched up her dress. Climbed onto the parapet. Threw herself into the water. She had gone through it all in her imagination: the way she would instinctively hold her breath as she jumped; the cold that would come over her; freeze her muscles; make her sink to the bottom.

Jules redid his bandage. The bagginess of his trousers allowed him free movement. He didn't think of putting on a jacket or coat. Went out in shirtsleeves. Warm body steaming in the winter cold. He was high; impatient at the thought of seeing her again. Anticipating being able to make her a woman; giving her this fabulous present. While tattooing, he had been wholly concentrated on doing a good job. Now, he called up memories; the smells, his hand brushing against the lace of her panties.

The moonlight was very clear. Stronger than the streetlamps. He walked without paying any attention to the occasional pedestrians who all turned back to look at him. It was one of the coldest nights since the beginning of winter. His body had stayed warm; there was a cloud of steam in his wake.

As he approached the Seine he became aware of a familiar smell cutting through the coldness of the air; but from where?

He recognised Angelina's dad on the Pont Marie. He was leaning on the parapet, crying. Much as he had known that this day might come, he was still suffused with grief. Jules looked up at the light in Angelina's window. Alfred's suffering told him it indicated her absence.

Orphan, Jules experienced these father's tears for his daughter as a kind of balm. He thought of all the tears that had made him a fighter. Knocked about for a yes; for a no. Even fathers could cry for their children. Jules tried to think of the word for a father or mother who had lost their child. He couldn't. He knew his vocabulary was limited, but he also knew that the word didn't exist. There were words for an orphan; for a widow or widower, but no name for the loss of a child. He felt like a son for the first time ever. His heart beat with the desire to father a child. But it was too late: what children could come from this shell?

Jules passed Alfred. Walked down the steps to the Quai d'Anjou. Now he could smell the scent properly; it was coming from the river. Alfred looked at the man in shirtsleeves, trailing a cloud of steam, calm and upright on the banks of the Seine. The man looking up at him. With so much love in his gaze. Was it an angel, he wondered? Especially when he saw him crouching down and slipping into the river, fully dressed.

"He's going to join Angelina, my little girl," he said to himself.

Jules was taken in a swirl of water. Oblivious to its cold. The smell of dead flesh flooded through him, giving him his bearings. He gave a great kick. Swam. Despite not knowing how to swim. Plunged downwards. Could see in the underwater night. As clear as day. Murdered people crowded on the river bed as far as the eye could see. They were all floating halfway down, weighted by the sandbags, stones, lumps of cast iron, copings and sinks attached to their feet. The Seine, graveyard of impunity; its residents hidden beneath the shiny surface. Hundreds of them; thousands. Standing there like ears of corn, leaning with the current. Jules felt his appetite quicken. Much as he tried to deny it, he was salivating.

Some of them were disintegrating: those killed before the winter. Hordes of small lively fish crowded round them. The cold had preserved the others almost intact. Above them, a drowned man was floating towards the ocean. Jules couldn't see Angelina. Had she sunk straight to the bottom? Or got stuck among these murder victims? Jules plunged deeper. Swam among them. Fast. Came face to face with Marcel, tied by his ankle to the family anchor. Jules fought the current to stay by his friend. OK, so they were friends, but from that to salivating over him? Jules no longer understood himself. He grabbed the chain holding Marcel down. Crushed it. The links broke in his hand. Marcel floated up to the surface. Just a vessel with its eyes closed. Drifting on its back. Past the Palais de Justice.

Jules swam off, hoping to escape this appetite for human flesh. But deep within he still felt as if he was swimming in an inexhaustible pantry.

Angelina's perfume cut through the bouquet of smells. Jules was intoxicated by his own strength. He sped past a barge hull, brown algae under the waterline, periodic bridge supports. Slime-clothed outlines of junked objects among the corpses heralded the beginnings of industrial vegetation.

Here was Angelina. She'd been swept along in the current. As white as a corpse. Jules caught her. Took her in his arms. Wrapped his legs around hers. Held her against him, feeling her breasts, hardened by the freezing water. His cock stiffened. He squeezed. His cock that was supposed to bring her to life. He squeezed. Her ribs cracked. He took her pelvis in his hands: squeezed it. Under her coat the bones snapped. His strength wasn't intentional. His hands let go; then squeezed again. They caught hold of and broke the legs; the feet; up again; crushed the spinal column; the shoulders; the arms; the hands. Reduced the bones to a pulp. Kneaded, until nothing hard was left. The body wasn't bleeding. Jules took hold of the head. The face disappeared between his palms. He hugged the flaccid body that desired only to slip from his hands. Undid the buttons of the dress, one at a time. Pulled up the blouse. Uncovered the tattoo. Bit into it. Sucked the fluid. Small fish rushed over, avid for any liquid leaking between the orifice and his mouth. He chased them away.

"A scavenger. I've become a scavenger," he said to himself, spooned against her.

At the bottom of the Seine, half-covered in slime, Jules uncurled himself. Angelina was only a shapeless skinbag now. Her face was no longer visible in her head. Mouth to the tattoo, he sucked once more.

Satisfied, he looked at his hands. To be sure, they were as strong as a lobster, but they were human hands. He opened his arms. Angelina's body slipped away. Fluid algae in the current. Sliding over the stiffs. A dribble of pulp leaked from the open tattoo, a host of fish in its wake.

Jules came to the surface. It was early morning. His head radiated a halo of steam on the Seine.

The smell of bay leaves spread throughout Paris.

ACKNOWLEDGEMENTS

Guillaume Lecasble would like to thank Geraldine D'Amico, Polly McLean and Maylis Vauterin without whom *Lobster* would never have crossed the channel.

CLUE BOOKS

Seashore Animals

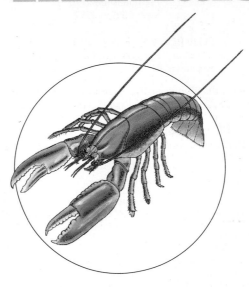

Gwen Allen   Joan Denslow

OXFORD UNIVERSITY PRESS

Oxford University Press, Great Clarendon Street, Oxford OX2 6DP

Oxford New York
Athens Auckland Bangkok Bogotá Bombay
Buenos Aires Calcutta Cape Town Dar es Salaam
Delhi Florence Hong Kong Istanbul Karachi
Kuala Lumpur Madras Madrid Melbourne
Mexico City Nairobi Paris Singapore
Taipei Tokyo Toronto

and associated companies in
Berlin Ibadan

Oxford is a trade mark of Oxford University Press

© Oxford University Press 1997
First published 1970
New edition 1997

CLUE BOOKS - SEASHORE ANIMALS
produced for Oxford University Press
by Bender Richardson White, Uxbridge

Editors: Lionel Bender, John Stidworthy   Design: Ben White
Media Conversion and Page Make-up: MW Graphics
Project Manager: Kim Richardson
Original artwork: Derek Whiteley
Additional artwork: Ron Hayward and Clive Pritchard

A CIP catalogue record for this book is available from the British Library

ISBN 0-19-910179-5 (hardback)
ISBN 0-19-910185-X (paperback)

1 3 5 7 9 10 8 6 4 2

Printed in Italy

Turn over stones and lift up seaweeds; watch to see what the animals under them are doing.

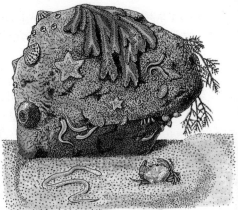

Do they move away quickly? Do they bury themselves in the sand or mud? Do they stay quite still so that they are difficult to see (camouflaged)? Do they make themselves look frightening? What else do they do?

an upturned rock

When you have found out what the animals are, you may like to record your observations in a pocket book or photograph them.

REMEMBER turn back the stones as you found them; otherwise many small animals may dry up and die before the tide comes in again.

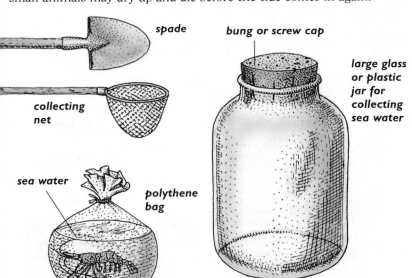

spade

collecting net

sea water

polythene bag

bung or screw cap

large glass or plastic jar for collecting sea water

When the tide is coming in, sit quietly, and watch the **LIMPETS** (see page 53) begin to move as the water covers them.

Which way do they move?
How fast do they travel?
Are they grazing as they go?

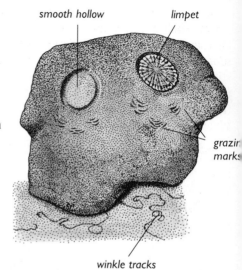

smooth hollow   limpet

grazing marks

winkle tracks

Look for:
1. The hollows in the rocks made by limpets. The limpets return to their own hollows when the tide goes out.

2. The grazing marks on rocks where limpets have scraped off tiny seaweeds with their *radulas* (see page 53).

3. **WINKLE** tracks in sandy pools.

adult Acorn Barnacle

Using a magnifying lens, watch **ACORN BARNACLES** (see page 64) when they are covered by the tide.

Watch animals feeding in rock pools and aquariums. How do they catch their food and eat it?

Shells and other dry specimens you have collected may be classified (grouped) and mounted either under clear self-adhesive plastic in a Seashore Book, or stuck in shallow boxes and covered with cellophane for protection.

The shells of many seashore animals are made of a chalky substance called calcium carbonate.

Test this by putting a drop of vinegar or dilute hydrochloric acid on an empty shell. If it is made of calcium carbonate, the liquid will bubble as it dissolves the shell and causes it to give off a gas (carbon dioxide). Use a lens to see the bubbles more clearly.

It is possible to tell the age of some animals by counting the growth rings on their scales or shells.

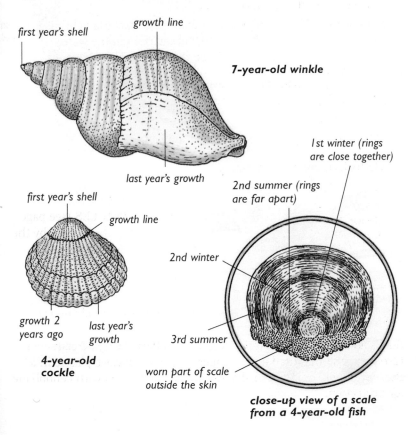

first year's shell

growth line

7-year-old winkle

last year's growth

first year's shell

growth line

growth 2 years ago

last year's growth

4-year-old cockle

1st winter (rings are close together)

2nd summer (rings are far apart)

2nd winter

3rd summer

worn part of scale outside the skin

close-up view of a scale from a 4-year-old fish

A FOOD WEB IN THE SEA

All plants and animals need food to supply energy for growing and moving. Seaweeds have a green pigment, called chlorophyll, as well as sometimes red or brown pigments, which traps the energy in sunlight and uses it to make food. Animals eat this ready-made food.

The animals that eat plants are called **HERBIVORES**. Those that eat other animals are called **CARNIVORES**. The **PLANKTON** (see page 18) is the most important supply of food in the sea.

SCAVENGERS feed on dead plants and animals: bacteria help to turn the waste materials into fertilizers that are carried in the water currents back to the plants, which use them again to make food.

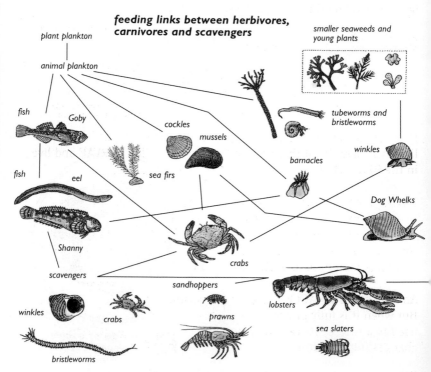

feeding links between herbivores, carnivores and scavengers

plant plankton

animal plankton

smaller seaweeds and young plants

fish

Goby

cockles

mussels

tubeworms and bristleworms

fish

eel

sea firs

barnacles

winkles

Dog Whelks

Shanny

scavengers

crabs

winkles

crabs

sandhoppers

prawns

lobsters

sea slaters

bristleworms

Most adult animals living in seawater lay eggs. Some of the eggs that you may find are illustrated on pages 18–21.

Many eggs hatch into young animals almost like their parents.

Rough Periwinkle eggs grow into young animals inside the parent's body.

young Rough Periwinkles

Flatfish eggs hatch into small fish: as they grow and become less active they rest at the bottom of the sea, lying on their left sides. Because the bones of the skull grow unequally, the left eye moves upwards until both eyes are on the same side.

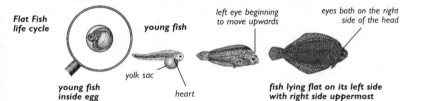

Flat Fish life cycle

young fish inside egg

yolk sac

young fish

heart

left eye beginning to move upwards

eyes both on the right side of the head

fish lying flat on its left side with right side uppermost

Many of the eggs hatch into young animals that do not at first look like their parents. At this stage of life they are called **LARVAE** and live in the **PLANKTON**.

LARVAE of the **CRUSTACEANS** (pages 64–69). These shed their skins (moult, see page 66) several times as they grow, and become more like their parents each time.

Crabs, Lobsters & Prawns

stage 1 *stage 2*

An **ACORN BARNACLE LARVA** is free-swimming. But when it is fully grown, it attaches itself to a rock by its cement glands and changes into an adult.

antennules

Acorn Barnacle Larva

When you have found an animal, the clues on pages 10–43 will help you to name it. Begin by using the clues on pages 10–17. Look carefully at the animal. If it is small, use a magnifying lens or microscope. Find the clue that fits it, then turn to the page given for the next clue. Repeat this until you find its name or group.

CLUES TO NAMING ANIMALS THAT LIVE ON THE SEASHORE

CLUE A

If the animal has fins, it is a **FISH**.

 4

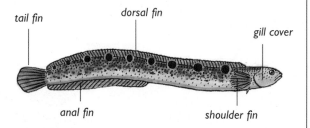

tail fin

dorsal fin

gill cover

anal fin

shoulder fin

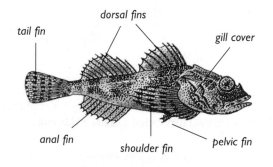

tail fin

dorsal fins

gill cover

anal fin

shoulder fin

pelvic fin

CLUE B | If the body and legs of the animal are covered with a hard or tough skin that has soft joints it is an **INSECT** or a **CRUSTACEAN**.

 34

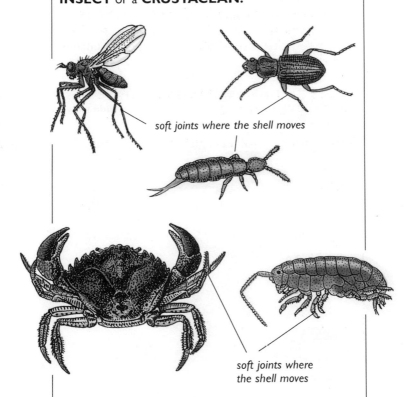

soft joints where the shell moves

soft joints where the shell moves

CLUE C | If the animal has a jointed leathery shell which is covered with long hairs but has no legs, it is probably a **BRISTLEWORM** called a **SEA MOUSE**.

 48

CLUE D If the animal has one or more hard shells, but no jointed legs

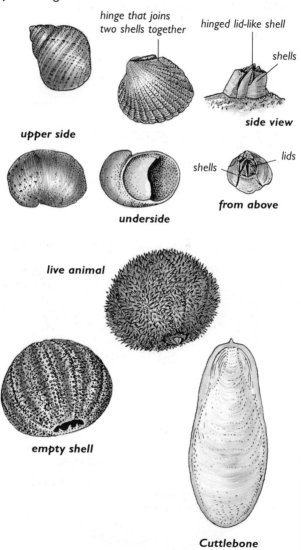

hinge that joins two shells together

hinged lid-like shell

shells

side view

upper side

shells

lids

from above

underside

live animal

empty shell

Cuttlebone

CLUE E

If the animal has several arms with many small feet underneath and is star-shaped, it is either a **STARFISH**, a **CUSHION STAR** or a **BRITTLESTAR** (types of ECHINODERMS).

71

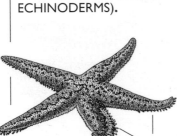

rows of tube feet

CLUE F

If the animal lives in a tube, it is a **BRISTLEWORM.**

48

white spiral tubes on seaweed or stone

smooth white tubes

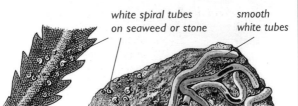

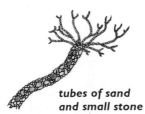

tubes of sand and small stone

tubes of sand

CLUE G If the animal is worm-like, it may be one of these

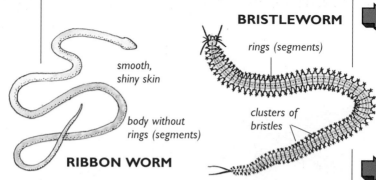

BRISTLEWORM

rings (segments)

smooth,
shiny skin

clusters of
bristles

body without
rings (segments)

RIBBON WORM

4

5

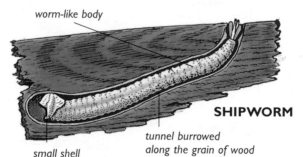

worm-like body

SHIPWORM

tunnel burrowed
along the grain of wood

small shell

CLUE H If the animal has several tentacles, it may be one of these

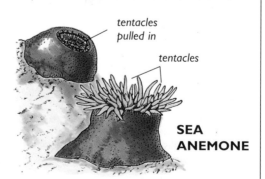

tentacles
pulled in

tentacles

**SEA
ANEMONE**

4

CLUE H
continued

RED THREAD or SAND MASON WORM

long slender tentacles

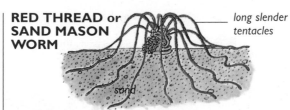

sand

 51

JELLYFISH

47

tentacles with suckers

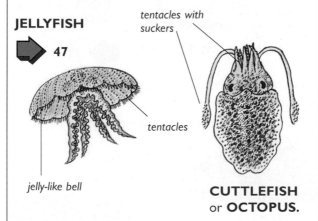

tentacles

jelly-like bell

CUTTLEFISH or OCTOPUS.

 61

CLUE I

If the animal is slug-like (put it into sea water to look at it), it may be a **SEA SLUG.**

 60

CLUE J   If the animal is oval-shaped, it may be one of these

PURSE SPONGE ➡ **47**

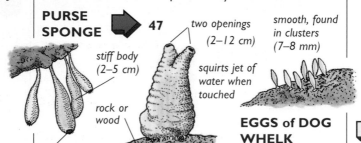

two openings (2–12 cm)

smooth, found in clusters (7–8 mm)

stiff body (2–5 cm)

squirts jet of water when touched

rock or wood

hairs around opening

EGGS of DOG WHELK

SEA SQUIRT ➡ **72**

CLUE K   If the animals form a spongy or slimy covering on rock surfaces, they may be one of these

BREADCRUMB SPONGE

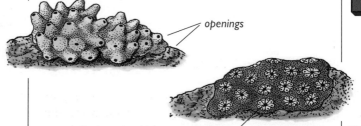

openings

hole through which water and food passes to the cluster of sea squirts

STAR SEA SQUIRT

CLUE L   If it is bony and looks like any of these, it may be a **FISH BONE**. Look at drawings of fish skeletons in a book about fish.

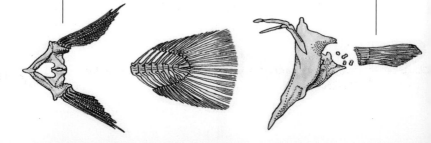

CLUE M | If it looks like one of these

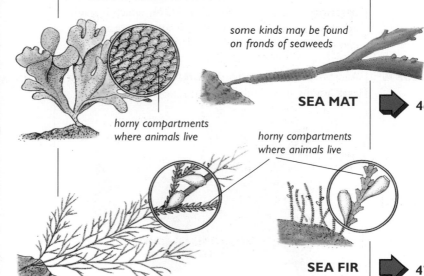

some kinds may be found on fronds of seaweeds

horny compartments where animals live

horny compartments where animals live

SEA MAT → 46

SEA FIR → 47

Beware: a **CORALLINE SEAWEED** may look like a **SEA FIR**.

Coralline Seaweed may be recognized by testing its hard covering in a little vinegar or dilute hydrochloric acid. If it is a seaweed the hard covering will dissolve and the soft seaweed inside will be left.

hard jointed stems

CLUE N | If your specimen is not like any of these, it may be **EGGS**.

 18

Many seawater animals lay minute eggs in the sea. The eggs float about in the **PLANKTON,** which is made up of numerous small plants, eggs and young animals (see page 9).

CLUE A All animals belonging to the **CRAB** group carry their eggs among their limbs.

6

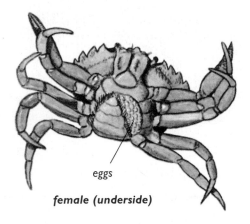

eggs

female (underside)

CLUE B Eggs may be attached under stones or to seaweeds low down on the shore.

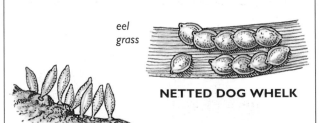

eel grass

NETTED DOG WHELK

rock

DOG WHELK

5

5

CLUE B
continued

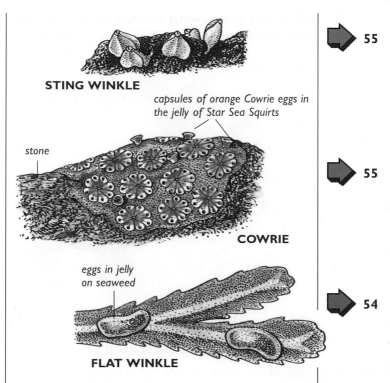

55

STING WINKLE

capsules of orange Cowrie eggs in the jelly of Star Sea Squirts

stone

55

COWRIE

eggs in jelly on seaweed

54

FLAT WINKLE

CLUE C

Many **FISH** lay masses of coloured eggs over rocks or attached to seaweeds. They are often guarded by the male fish.

74

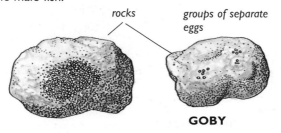

rocks

groups of separate eggs

GOBY

CLUE D

EGGS laid in deep water are often washed ashore or left in rock pools by the tide.

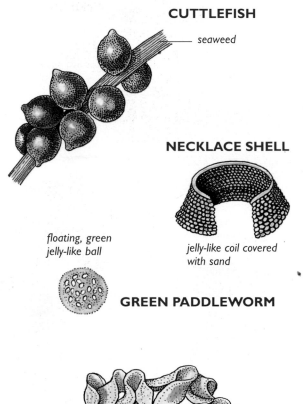

CUTTLEFISH

seaweed

NECKLACE SHELL

floating, green jelly-like ball

jelly-like coil covered with sand

GREEN PADDLEWORM

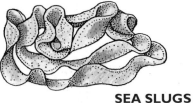

SEA SLUGS

Most Sea Slugs lay jelly-like ribbons of eggs amongst seaweed low on the shore.

CLUE E | Empty **EGG CASES**

 52

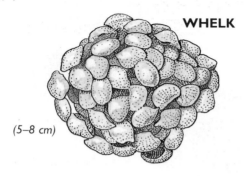

WHELK

(5–8 cm)

egg case of Skate or Ray
(5–15 cm)

egg case of Dogfish
(5–10 cm)

The egg cases of Skates, Rays and Dogfish are often called Mermaids' Purses. These fish live in coastal waters (so are not featured in this book). You may find their skeletons washed up on the seashore.

CLUE A

If the shell has several parts and looks like this, it is an **ACORN BARNACLE**.

lid (moveable shell)

side view

seen from above

6

CLUE B

If the shell is almost flat, has several parts, and the animal has a flat muscular foot, it is a **CHITON** (Coat of Mail).

5

CLUE C

If the shell is solid, white, very light in weight and crumbles when scratched, it is a **CUTTLEFISH** shell (often called a 'bone').

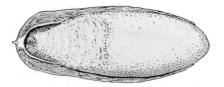

6

WHAT KIND OF SHELL?

CLUE D | If the shell is oval, has a plate of shell half way across inside, and is often found in clusters, it is a **SLIPPER LIMPET**.

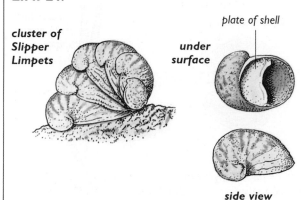

cluster of Slipper Limpets

plate of shell

under surface

side view

CLUE E | If the shell is more or less spherical and has a round hole in the under surface, it is an **URCHIN**.

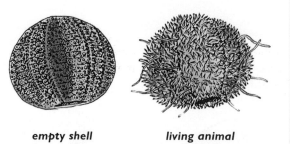

empty shell

living animal

CLUE F

If there are two shells hinged together, or a single shell showing a hinge mark it is a **MOLLUSC.**

2

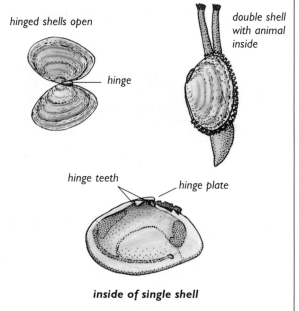

hinged shells open

hinge

double shell with animal inside

hinge teeth   *hinge plate*

inside of single shell

CLUE G

If the single shell is shaped like one of these it is a **MOLLUSC.**

2

General information about one-shelled molluscs can be found on page 52.

CLUE A | If the shell is shaped like a cone, it is a **LIMPET**. 53

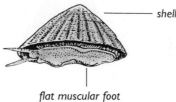

shell

flat muscular foot

CLUE B | If the shell is oval and the opening is a long narrow slit, it is a **COWRIE**. 55

CLUE C | If the shell is spiral  26

CLUE D

If the worn shell shows a pearly layer, is very flat below, and the animal has several tentacles around the foot, it may be a **TOP SHELL.**

5

tentacles

spirally marked operculum

foot

CLUE E

If the shell is long and narrow, it may be a **TOWER SHELL.**

5

CLUE F | If the shell has a large first whorl, rows of dark spots and is very smooth and shiny, it may be a **NECKLACE SHELL**.

 55

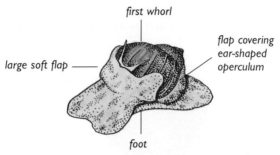

first whorl

flap covering ear-shaped operculum

large soft flap

foot

CLUE G | If the edge of the shell is folded to form a notch in the front, it is a **WHELK**.

52, 55

notch

notch for siphon

operculum

CLUE H | If the shell does not have a notch, it may be a **WINKLE**.

 54

General information about two-shelled molluscs can
be found on page 56.

CLUE A   If the shell is irregular in shape, thick, has a bumpy
surface, is dull outside and pearly inside, it is a **FLAT
OYSTER**.

5■

upper shell

CLUE B   If the shell is nearly circular, dull, white or pinkish
outside and pearly inside, it is a **SADDLE OYSTER**.

5■

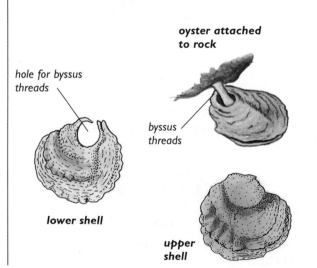

*oyster attached
to rock*

*hole for byssus
threads*

*byssus
threads*

lower shell

*upper
shell*

CLUE C

If the shell is long, narrow and smooth, it is a **RazOR SHELL.**

 59

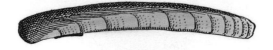

CLUE D

If the shell is oval with ridges, has a tooth-like edge and is found in holes in rock, it is a **PIDDOCK.**

 58

tooth-like edge

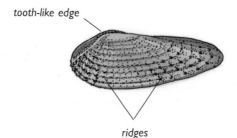

ridges

CLUE E

If the shell is rounded with ear-like pieces at the hinge end and is sometimes flat, it is a **SCALLOP.**

 58

CLUE F

If the shell is ridged from top to bottom and is shaped like this, it is a **COCKLE.**

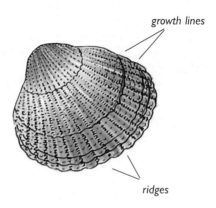

growth lines

ridges

 5

CLUE G

If the shell is dark blue and triangular, it is a **MUSSEL.** Mussels are found in large numbers on the shore, especially where fresh water enters the sea (for example, in an estuary).

 5

UE H

If the shell is not like those on pages 28 to 30, examine it closely, using a lens if possible. Examine the teeth inside the hinge of the shell.

If the shell is thick, nearly circular, has many teeth and is covered with brown markings, it is a **DOG COCKLE.**

 58

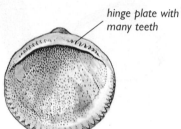

hinge plate with many teeth

inside of shell

UE I

If the shells are thick, oval, often darkly coloured, gape (do not fit together) behind and have a flat hinge shelf on the left shell that fits a gristle pad on the right shell, it is a **GAPER.**

 59

hollow pad that fits over the gristle pad

ends of the shells that do not touch when the shells are together

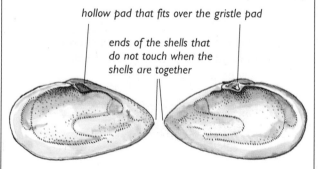

CLUE J

If the shell is thick with well-marked growth lines, has a lunule (a heart-shaped patch of smooth shell near the hinge) and three or four hinge teeth, it is a **VENUS**.

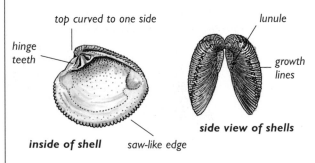

top curved to one side

lunule

hinge teeth

growth lines

inside of shell

saw-like edge

side view of shells

CLUE K

If the shell has teeth and a lunule like a Venus but the shell and its edge are smooth, it is an **ARTEMIS**.

CLUE L

If the shell has teeth like a Venus but no lunule, it may be a **CARPET SHELL**.

CLUE M

If the shell is pale, thin, flattened, and shiny with not more than two teeth, and often found still joined in pairs, it may be a **TELLIN**.

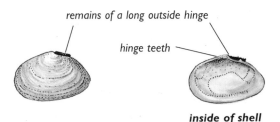

remains of a long outside hinge

hinge teeth

inside of shell

LUE N

If the shell is oval, very shiny, brown, yellow or violet with violet marks inside, has two short central and two long side teeth, it is a **BANDED WEDGE SHELL.**

 59

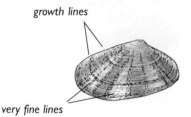

growth lines

very fine lines

hinge teeth ——

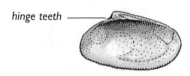

inside of shell

LUE O

If the shell is flattened, triangular and has 4 to 6 well-marked teeth, it is a **TROUGH SHELL.**

 58

hinge teeth

inside of shell

CLUE A If the animal has six jointed legs and wings, it may be an **INSECT** visiting the shore to scavenge for food.

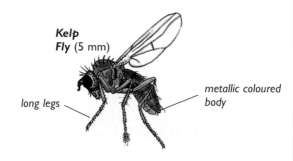

*Kelp
Fly* (5 mm)

long legs

*metallic coloured
body*

*very
short,
hard
wing
cases*

*long
slender
antenna*

*hard wing
cases*

Rove Beetle
(10 mm)

Ground Beetle (8 mm)

CLUE B If the animal has six jointed legs and no wings, it may be either an **INSECT**

*does not
jump*

Bristletail (17 mm)

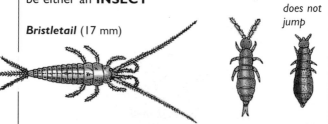

Springtails (3 mm)

LUE B
ontinued

or a **LARVA** of the **CRAB GROUP.**

 5

jointed limbs

LUE C

If the animal has ten or more jointed legs, it belongs to the **CRAB GROUP** (CRUSTACEA).

 36

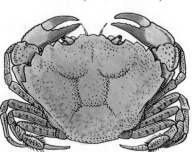

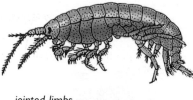

jointed limbs

shell

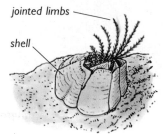

General information about Crustaceans can be found
on page 64.

CLUE A If the body of the animal
is flattened from top to
bottom and all the legs
are alike

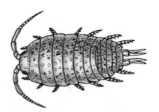

3

CLUE B If the animal has long walking legs and small limbs
called swimmerets

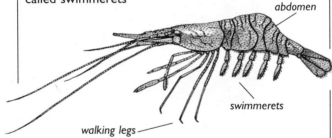

abdomen

swimmerets

walking legs

3

CLUE C If the animal has five pairs of legs and its abdomen
and swimmerets are tucked under its body it is a
CRAB.

6
7

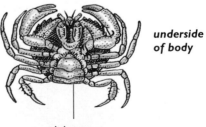

*underside
of body*

*abdomen
turned back*

LUE D | If the animal has one large and one small pincer, a soft abdomen and lives in a winkle or whelk shell, it is a **HERMIT CRAB.**

66,
69

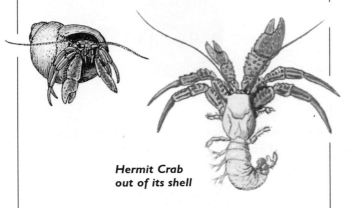

*Hermit Crab
out of its shell*

LUE E | If the animal looks like this, it is an **ACORN BARNACLE.**

67

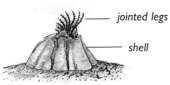

jointed legs

shell

CLUE A | If the animal rolls into a ball, it may be a **PILL BUG.**

If the animal does not roll into a ball, it may be a **SEA SLATER.**

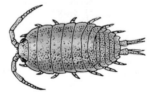

CLUE B | If the animal has eyes on short stalks, it may be a **CRAWFISH, PRAWN** or **SHRIMP**

stalked eye

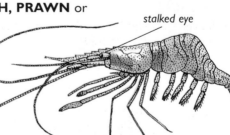

6

6

6

CLUE B
continued

or it may be a **LOBSTER.**

 67

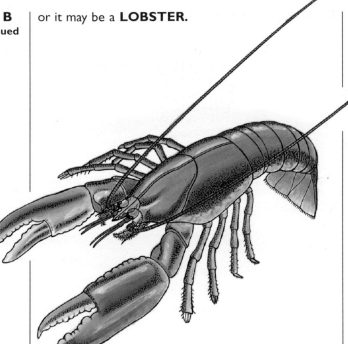

If the animal is small and its eyes are not stalked, it may be a **SANDHOPPER.**

67

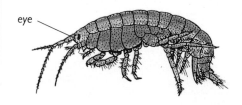

eye

CLUE A
General information about fish can be found on page 74.
If the fish has a long thin body with a single fin most of the way round, it is an **EEL** or a **SAND EEL.**

 7

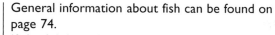

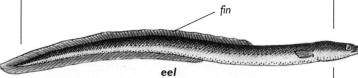

fin

eel

CLUE B
If the fish has a long thin body and a separate tail fin

 4

tail fin

CLUE C
If the fish has a body that is not as long or thin, but is rounded

 4

CLUE D
If the fish has a body that is flattened, it is a **FLATFISH,** and may be either a **DAB** or **PLAICE.**

 7

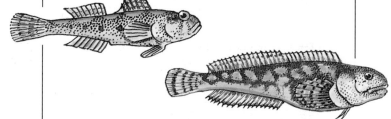

From page
0 clues B, C

CLUE A

If the fish has a stiff body covered with bony plates, it is a **PIPE FISH**.

 76

If the fish is very smooth and slippery and has black spots down its back, it is a **BUTTERFISH** (GUNNEL).

 79

If the fish has no spots and the lower jaw is longer than the upper, it is a **SAND EEL**.

 79

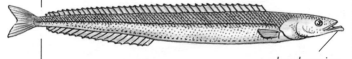

long lower jaw

CLUE B

If the fish has one dorsal fin   *dorsal fin*

 42

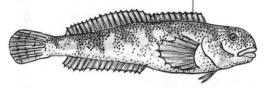

If the fish has two dorsal fins   *dorsal fins*

43

dorsal fins

CLUE A | If the fish has barbels, it may be a **ROCKLING.**

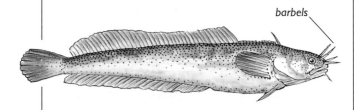

barbels

CLUE B | If the fish has a sucker underneath, it may be a **SUCKERFISH.**

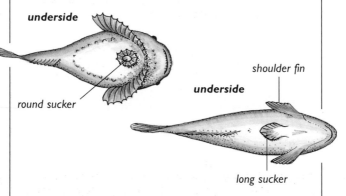

underside

round sucker

shoulder fin

underside

long sucker

CLUE C | If the fish has a large head and large shoulder fins, it may be a **BLENNY.**

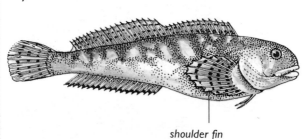

shoulder fin

CLUE A | If the fish has a sucker underneath and large eyes, it is a **GOBY**.

76

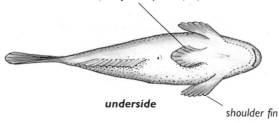

sucker (two joined pelvic fins)

underside

shoulder fin

CLUE B | If the front dorsal fin is made up of many separate spines, it is a **STICKLEBACK**.

76

CLUE C | If the fish is spiny, looks like this and lives on rocky shores, it may be a **BULLHEAD** (SEA SCORPION).

77

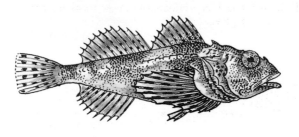

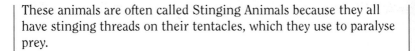
These animals are often called Stinging Animals because they all have stinging threads on their tentacles, which they use to paralyse prey.

They all produce eggs which, when fertilized, typically hatch into simple, oval larvae covered in tiny, hair-like cilia.

SEA ANEMONES sometimes produce tiny anemones like themselves as well. These escape through their mouths. These free-swimming anemones are covered in tiny hairs called cilia, but once they attach themselves to a surface they develop tentacles and live as adult anemones.

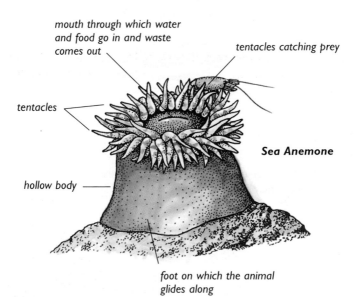

mouth through which water
and food go in and waste
comes out

tentacles catching prey

tentacles

Sea Anemone

hollow body

foot on which the animal
glides along

SEA FIRS are made up of tiny anemone-like animals living together in horny cases that they make as they grow.

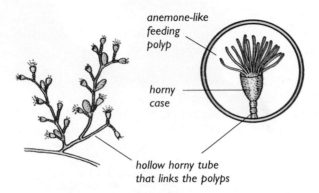

anemone-like
feeding
polyp

horny
case

hollow horny tube
that links the polyps

The larvae of **JELLYFISH** become attached to rocks and divide into rings as they grow. In late spring and autumn the rings separate one at a time, turn over, and become new jellyfish.

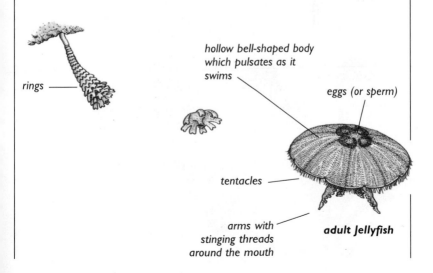

rings

hollow bell-shaped body
which pulsates as it
swims

eggs (or sperm)

tentacles

arms with
stinging threads
around the mouth

adult Jellyfish

in water

out of water

Beadlet Anemone
(column up to 7 cm tall)
mid and lower shore rocks

Snakelock Anemone
(column up to 4 cm)
mid and lower shore, on rocks; tentacles do not retract when out of water

SEA MATS (POLYZOA)

Hornwrack
(10–15 cm)
cast ashore from deep water

growing on base of seaweed stem

Jellyfish (7–20 cm)
float in the sea

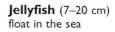

Sea Fir
(3–20 cm)
on rocks and
seaweeds
lower shore

SPONGES (PORIFERA)
under surface of rocks, lower shore

**Purse
Sponge**
(2–5 cm)

Breadcrumb Sponge
(patches 30–40 cm across)

BRISTLEWORMS

Many bristleworms wriggle about rapidly in pools or in wet sand, breathing through their skin.
They most often scavenge for food.

Other bristleworms live in tubes in the sand or on rocks. All bristleworms shed eggs and sperm into the sea.

The bristles of the **SEA MOUSE**, which are long and iridescent, cover its body.

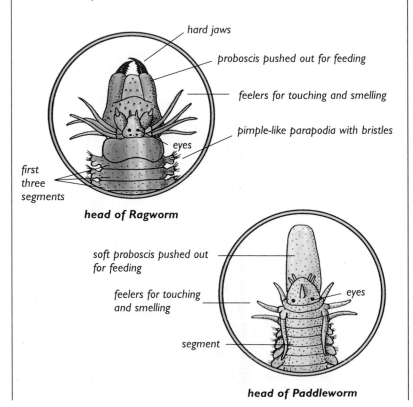

hard jaws

proboscis pushed out for feeding

feelers for touching and smelling

pimple-like parapodia with bristles

eyes

first
three
segments

head of Ragworm

soft proboscis pushed out
for feeding

feelers for touching
and smelling

eyes

segment

head of Paddleworm

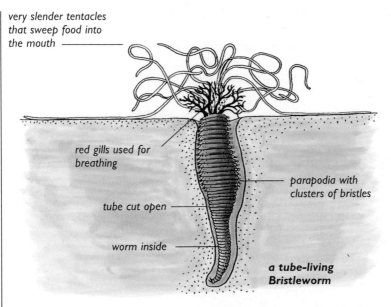

very slender tentacles that sweep food into the mouth

red gills used for breathing

parapodia with clusters of bristles

tube cut open

worm inside

a tube-living Bristleworm

LUGWORMS feed by digesting plant and animal material from the sand they swallow. Fishermen use them for bait.

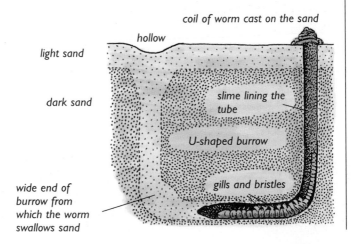

coil of worm cast on the sand

hollow

light sand

dark sand

slime lining the tube

U-shaped burrow

gills and bristles

wide end of burrow from which the worm swallows sand

RIBBON WORMS (worms without bristles)

Pink Ribbon Worm (3 cm)

under stones, lower shore, feed on bristleworms

Bootlace Worm (30–40 cm)

BRISTLEWORMS

Free-living Bristleworms

burrows in sand **Ragworm**
(2–25 cm)

Sea Mouse (7–10 cm)

deep sea, washed ashore

Green Paddleworm (3–10 cm)

among rocks, middle and lower shore; feeds on barnacles

Tube-living Bristleworms

Red Thread Worm
(2–10 cm)
slimy tubes; under stones;
lower shore

Sand Mason
(tube 30 cm)
in sandy tubes under
stones and among
sandy shingle;
lower shore

Peacock worm
(tube 45 cm)
in sand,
lower shore

Honeycomb Worms (2–4 cm)
mass of sandy tubes; on rocks
in sheltered bays

Serpulid Worms (1–15 cm)
in slimy tubes on rocks and
seaweeds over the shore

All one-shelled molluscs have a long tongue, called a radula, which is covered with many rows of teeth (see page 53). As the front teeth wear out, the tongue and teeth from behind move forward to take their place.

Most sea molluscs need to keep damp when the tide goes out. Many of them go into their shells and close the opening with an operculum; others move about under wet seaweed (see pages 7, 8).

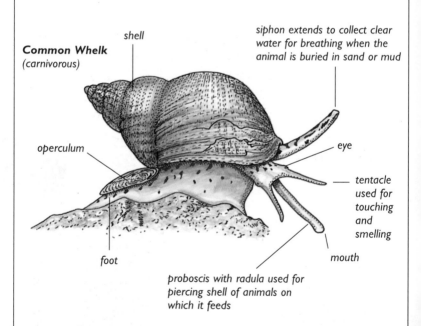

shell

Common Whelk
(carnivorous)

siphon extends to collect clear water for breathing when the animal is buried in sand or mud

operculum

eye

tentacle used for touching and smelling

foot

mouth

proboscis with radula used for piercing shell of animals on which it feeds

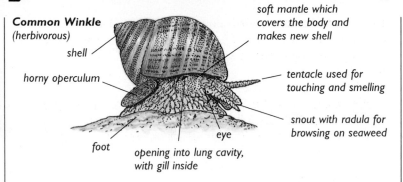

Common Winkle
(herbivorous)

shell

horny operculum

foot

opening into lung cavity,
with gill inside

eye

soft mantle which
covers the body and
makes new shell

tentacle used for
touching and smelling

snout with radula for
browsing on seaweed

CHITONS and LIMPETS cling tightly to the rocks when the tide is out.

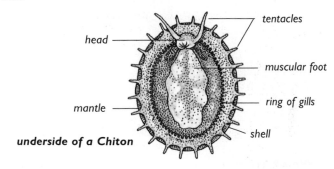

head

mantle

tentacles

muscular foot

ring of gills

shell

underside of a Chiton

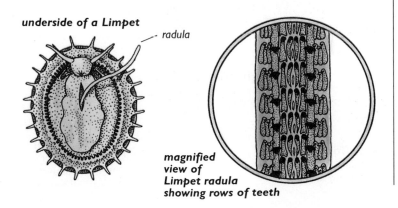

underside of a Limpet

radula

*magnified
view of
Limpet radula
showing rows of teeth*

These below feed on seaweeds on rocky shores

Limpet (up to 7 cm long)
on rocks

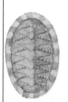

Chiton (1–2 cm)
beneath rocks

Common Winkle
(25 mm)
edible, middle and
lower shore

Flat Topshell (13 mm)
lower shore

Painted Topshell (25 mm)
lower shore

Flat Winkle (10 mm)
middle and lower
shore

Rough Winkle (8 mm)
upper and
middle shore

Grey Topshell
(13 mm)
middle and lower shore

Tower Shell
(4–6 cm)
deep water shell
washed ashore

These below feed on animals

Necklace Shell (15 mm)
lower shady shore; bores
holes into bivalve shells

eggs

Cowrie (12 mm)
lower shore; feeds
on Star Sea Squirts

Slipper Limpet (3 cm)
sheltered shores; filters
small animals from seawater

Sting Winkle (5 cm)
lower shore;
feeds on other molluscs

**Netted Dog
Whelk** (3 cm)
lower shore and
below; feeds on
other molluscs

Common Whelk (10 cm)
lower shore and below; burrows
in mud or sand; feeds on other
molluscs and scavenges

egg capsules

Dog Whelks (3 cm)
rocky shores; feed on
barnacles and mussels

Most two-shelled (bivalve) molluscs that live on the seashore
burrow in sand. When the tide is high they collect water through
their siphons which stretch as they go deeper.

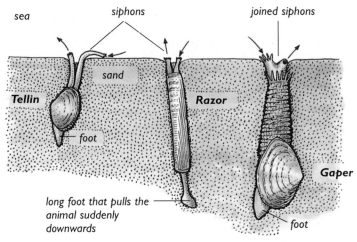

sea

siphons

joined siphons

sand

Tellin

foot

Razor

Gaper

long foot that pulls the
animal suddenly
downwards

foot

PIDDOCKS burrow into
rocks; the see-saw movements
of their rough shells wear
away the rocks. When the tide
is out Piddocks squirt jets of
water from their siphons.

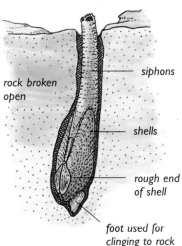

rock broken
open

siphons

shells

rough end
of shell

foot used for
clinging to rock

The seawater contains oxygen for breathing and food (decaying plant and animal material) which is carried by hair-like cilia on the gills to their mouths.

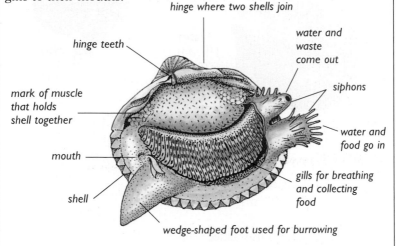

hinge where two shells join

hinge teeth

water and waste come out

siphons

mark of muscle that holds shell together

water and food go in

mouth

gills for breathing and collecting food

shell

wedge-shaped foot used for burrowing

inside of a Cockle
the second shell has been removed

SCALLOPS are sensitive to approaching prey and suddenly close their shells, forcing out spurts of water which move them away quickly: done several times they appear to be swimming.

COCKLES, MUSSELS and SCALLOPS all have edible soft tissues.

Shells attached to rocks

upper shell

byssus threads

Oyster
(10 cm)
creeks and
estuaries

Mussel
(10 cm)
middle
and lower
shore

*hole for
byssus
threads*

Saddle Oyster
(up to 6 cm)
middle shore and below

upper shell   **lower shell**

Deep sea animals; shells washed ashore

Dog Cockle
(6 cm)

Trough Shell
(8 cm)

Scallop
(13 cm)

Makes holes in rocks

Piddock
(5–8 cm)

Makes deep burrows in sand

Tellin (2–6 cm)

Make shallow burrows in sand

Banded Wedge Shell (3 cm)

Cockle (6 cm)

Carpet Shell (2–5 cm)

Venus (4 cm)

Artemis (5 cm)

Make deep burrows in sand

Razor Shell (10–20 cm)

Gaper (12 cm)

SEA SLUGS

When sea slugs are seen in water they are brightly coloured animals. They lay ribbons of eggs in pools on the shore in spring (see page 20).

Some sea slugs look like this:

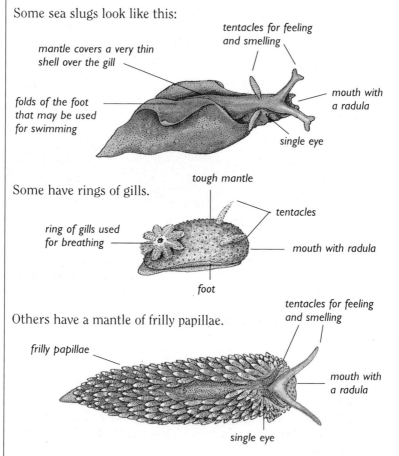

tentacles for feeling and smelling

mantle covers a very thin shell over the gill

mouth with a radula

folds of the foot that may be used for swimming

single eye

Some have rings of gills.

tough mantle

tentacles

ring of gills used for breathing

mouth with radula

foot

Others have a mantle of frilly papillae.

tentacles for feeling and smelling

frilly papillae

mouth with a radula

single eye

When frightened **SEA HARES** eject a purple liquid that hides them as they escape.

OCTOPUS, CUTTLEFISH and SQUID

These animals may be washed ashore in rough weather.
They are carnivorous and grip their food with the suckers on their
tentacles. The octopus has eight tentacles, with two rows of suckers
on each. Squid and cuttlefish have ten tentacles. Two are longer
than the others, with suckers only on the end pad.

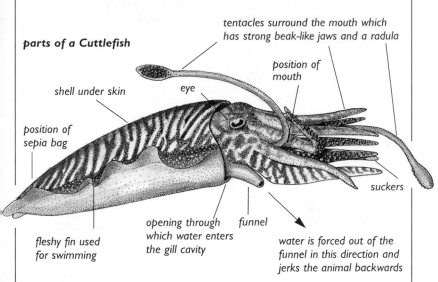

parts of a Cuttlefish

*tentacles surround the mouth which
has strong beak-like jaws and a radula*

*position of
mouth*

shell under skin

eye

*position of
sepia bag*

suckers

*fleshy fin used
for swimming*

*opening through
which water enters
the gill cavity*

funnel

*water is forced out of the
funnel in this direction and
jerks the animal backwards*

When they swim the tentacles are stretched out in front of the
mouth.
Their eggs (see page 20) hatch into young like their parents.

When these animals are frightened or move into differently
coloured surroundings, dark and light waves appear to move
through the skin as they rapidly change colour. They all have a bag
of dark liquid, called sepia, which they can eject to hide them while
they swim away.

Their eyes are large and similar to human eyes.

SEA SLUGS

jelly-like ribbon of Sea Slug eggs

Smooth Sea Slug (1 cm)
rocky shores; feeds on
green seaweeds

Sea Hare (15 cm)
among rocks low on shore;
feeds on seaweeds

Sea Lemon (5–7 cm)
among rocks low on shore;
feeds on Breadcrumb Sponge

Grey Sea Slug (6–8 cm)
under rocks, middle and lower
shore; feeds on sea anemones

Octopus (25 cm)
among oarweeds; deep pools; under rocks

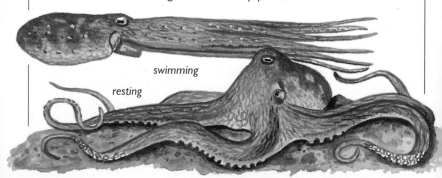

swimming

resting

Cuttlefish (30 cm)
deep water under
rocks and piers

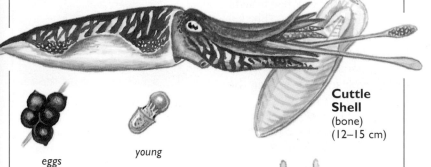

**Cuttle
Shell**
(bone)
(12–15 cm)

eggs

young

Little Cuttle (5 cm)
burrows in sand low on the shore

Common Squid (20–30 cm)
(rarely seen near shore)

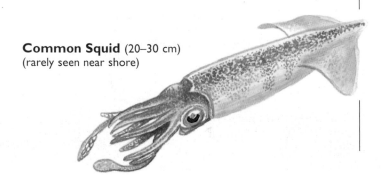

INSECTS

SPRINGTAILS and **BRISTLETAILS**
are among the very few insects
that live on the shore. They keep
dry and can even breathe under
water because air is trapped in
the hairs on their bodies.
They both scavenge among the
jetsam on the shore.

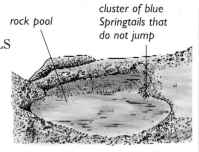

rock pool

cluster of blue
Springtails that
do not jump

Springtails may be seen in clusters on the surface of small pools
high up on the shore. Bristletails live in cracks in rocks above high
tide level. On sunny days, with the help of their long bristle tail,
they jump about on the rocks.

CRUSTACEANS

Many crustaceans are carnivores; they also scavenge.

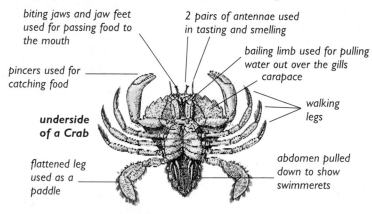

biting jaws and jaw feet
used for passing food to
the mouth

2 pairs of antennae used
in tasting and smelling

bailing limb used for pulling
water out over the gills
carapace

pincers used for
catching food

walking
legs

**underside
of a Crab**

flattened leg
used as a
paddle

abdomen pulled
down to show
swimmerets

BARNACLES use their feathery
limbs to filter small animals
from the water.

legs used
in feeding

moveable
lid

Barnacle

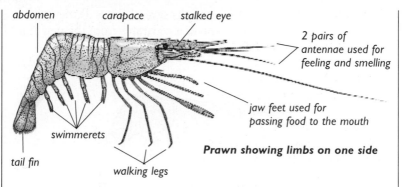

abdomen   *carapace*   *stalked eye*

2 pairs of antennae used for feeling and smelling

jaw feet used for passing food to the mouth

Prawn showing limbs on one side

swimmerets

tail fin

walking legs

Most crustaceans breathe through gills that spread out beneath the carapace. Water is kept moving over the gills, coming in between the carapace and the top of each leg, and being pulled out of the gill cavity by the movements of the bailing limb.

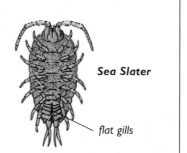

carapace cut away to show the gills on one side   *gills*   *abdomen*

bailing limb which pulls water out of gill cavity

water goes into gill cavity

head section of Prawn

SEA SLATERS and **PILL BUGS** have flat gills beneath the abdomen.

The females of many crustaceans carry their eggs among their swimmerets.

SLATERS and **SANDHOPPERS** carry their eggs in pouches among their walking legs.

Sea Slater

flat gills

All crustaceans shed their skins (moult) several times as they grow. When the shell is too small for them, it separates from the new skin below and splits across the back.

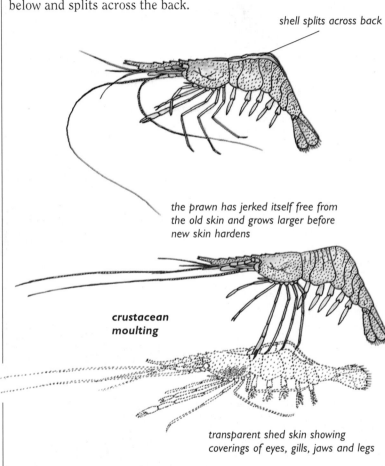

shell splits across back

the prawn has jerked itself free from the old skin and grows larger before new skin hardens

crustacean moulting

transparent shed skin showing coverings of eyes, gills, jaws and legs

The soft bodies of **HERMIT CRABS** are protected by the mollusc shell in which they live. They change the shell for a larger one as they grow.

Sea Slater (up to 3 cm) high on the shore under stones

Pill Bug (15 mm) high on the shore under stones

Acorn Barnacles (15 mm) on rocks

Sandhoppers dry sand high on the shore; jump among jetsam low down on the shore; wriggle about under stones

(up to 25 mm)   (15 mm)   (15 mm)   (6 mm)

Lobster (20–50 cm) among rocks in deep water

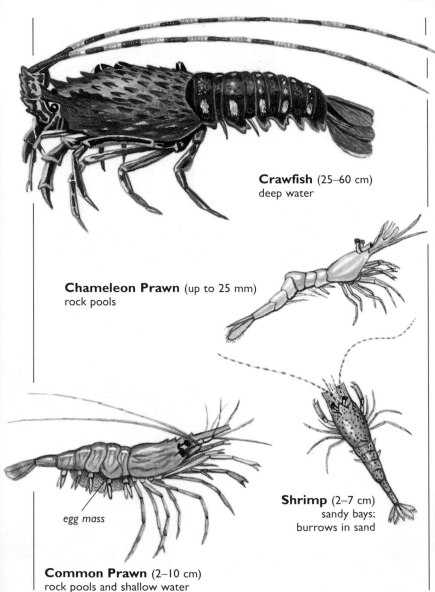

Crawfish (25–60 cm)
deep water

Chameleon Prawn (up to 25 mm)
rock pools

Shrimp (2–7 cm)
sandy bays;
burrows in sand

egg mass

Common Prawn (2–10 cm)
rock pools and shallow water

Hermit Crab (2–8 cm)
rock pools, among rocks at low tide;
keeps soft, curled abdomen in empty
shell, often, as here, a whelk shell;
changes shell home as grows.

Long-Clawed Porcelain Crab
(shell only 6 mm) under stones on
lower shore, clings flat against rock.

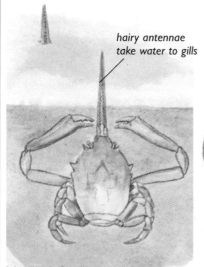

*hairy antennae
take water to gills*

Spiny Spider Crab
(5–18 cm) sand among
rocks and seaweeds, lower
shore; back often covered
with weeds or sponges.

Masked Crab
(shell 4 cm long) usually buried in sand,
lower shore; hairy antennae held together
as pipe to take water to gills.

Shore Crab (2–10 cm)
among seaweed, under stones, rock pools; from upper shore
downwards; green or brown; may run if disturbed; abdomen
curled under body, may be holding eggs in female (seen here from
below); male has smaller, pointed abdomen.

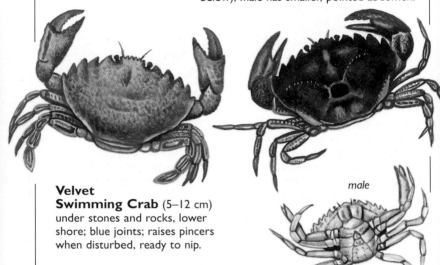

**Velvet
Swimming Crab** (5–12 cm)
under stones and rocks, lower
shore; blue joints; raises pincers
when disturbed, ready to nip.

male

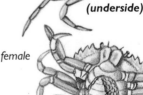

(underside)

female

eggs

(underside)

Edible Crab (5–25 cm)
under rocks and seaweed,
lower shore; black tips to
pincers; 'piecrust' edge to
shell; often folds in legs
when disturbed.

Most echinoderms have spiny skins and rows of water-filled tube feet, which most often have sucker ends. Echinoderms may use their tube feet to crawl about the seabed. They also use them for feeling and breathing. Some, especially those round the mouth, are used for smelling. Eggs and sperm are shed into the sea in spring.

STARFISH are carnivores. They use their strong arms with tube feet to open mussels and other shellfish. They then push their stomach out through the mouth to digest the soft body inside the shell.

BRITTLESTARS and **URCHINS** feed on small animals and plants. Starfish and Brittlestars often shed their arms when caught, but new arms grow to replace them.

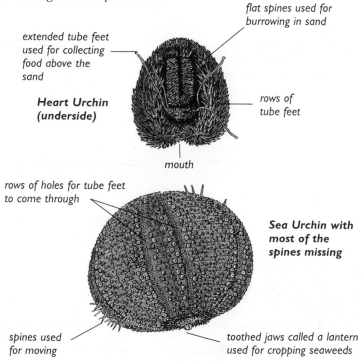

flat spines used for
burrowing in sand

extended tube feet
used for collecting
food above the
sand

**Heart Urchin
(underside)**

rows of
tube feet

mouth

rows of holes for tube feet
to come through

**Sea Urchin with
most of the
spines missing**

spines used
for moving

toothed jaws called a lantern
used for cropping seaweeds

Starfish (10–50 cm)
deep water
opening a mussel shell

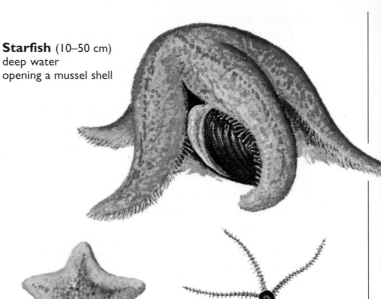

Cushion Star (2–10 cm)
on rocks near low water

Brittlestar (arms 2–15 cm)
under rocks low on shore

SEA SQUIRTS (TUNICATA)

Sea Squirt (2–12 cm)
on rocks, shells and piers;
lower shore

empty shell

Sea Urchin (7–10 cm) on rocks and sand in deep water

empty shell

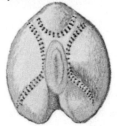

Heart Urchin (Sea Potato) (4–6 cm)
buried in sand; middle or lower shore

Star Sea Squirt (patches 1–15 cm across)
under surface of rocks;
lower shore

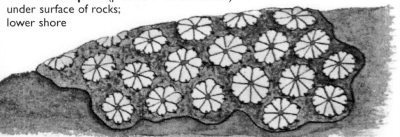

Many sea fish have scales in their skin; the slime on their bodies comes from glands in the skin. Look at a scale under good magnification. The number of rings on the scale give the approximate age of the fish (see page 7).

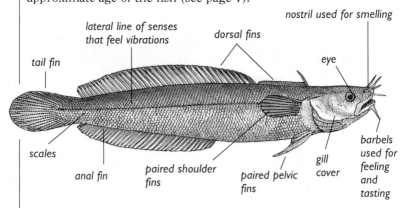

nostril used for smelling

lateral line of senses
that feel vibrations

dorsal fins

tail fin

eye

scales

barbels
used for
feeling
and
tasting

anal fin

paired shoulder
fins

paired pelvic
fins

gill
cover

All fish bolt their food without chewing it. Nearly all sea fish are carnivores; most of them have backward pointing teeth to prevent their prey escaping when caught.

SHANNIES have short, strong teeth which they use for biting barnacles and mussels off rocks.

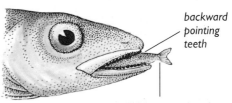

backward
pointing
teeth

small fish trapped in the
backward pointing teeth

The jaws of the **PIPEFISH** are joined to form a tube through which they suck very tiny animals from the seawater.

tube-like jaws
used for
sucking in
very tiny
animals

Fish breathe by taking oxygen from the water. As a fish opens and closes its mouth it takes in water, but instead of swallowing it, pushes it over the gills and out under the gill cover. The oxygen from the water passes through the skin of the gills into the blood of the fish. Waste carbon dioxide passes out into the water and is carried away.

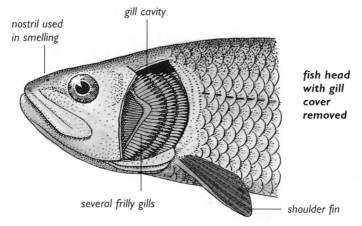

nostril used in smelling

gill cavity

fish head with gill cover removed

several frilly gills

shoulder fin

Many fish are difficult to see in their natural surroundings because they are camouflaged by their colour and their markings.

Some fish change their colour to match their surroundings.

a Plaice on a dark background

the Plaice, a few seconds later, swimming over a pale background

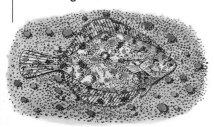

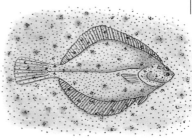

Worm Pipefish
(10–22 cm)
rocky coasts,
under weeds
and stones

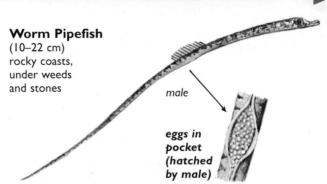

male

**eggs in
pocket
(hatched
by male)**

Stickleback (6–17 cm)
rocky coasts and pools

Common Goby (5–8 cm)
lie, partly buried in sand, in shallow water

Spotted Goby
(7 cm)
swim in shoals among seaweeds

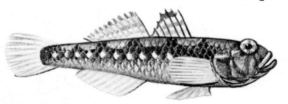

**Bullhead
(Sea Scorpion)**
(12–17 cm)

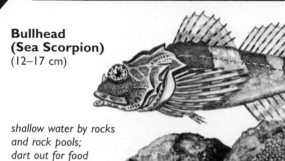

*shallow water by rocks
and rock pools;
dart out for food*

eggs

Plaice (7–40 cm)
shallow water of bays
and estuaries; often
partly buried in sand

Dab (7–25 cm)

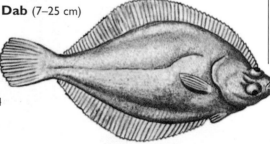

shallow water of
sandy bays, often
partly buried in sand

These are able to move easily among rocks and weeds

SMALL SCALES

Five Bearded Rockling (30–45 cm)
under stones and weeds at low tide

Common Blenny (Shanny) (7–12 cm)
rock pools

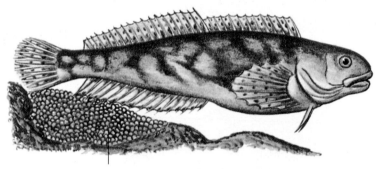

eggs

NO SCALES

Two-spot Sucker (5 cm)
under rocks
on shore in
summer

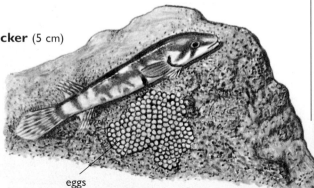

eggs

SMALL SCALES

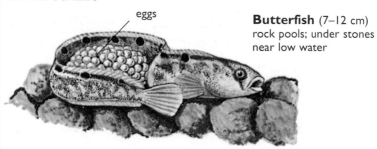

eggs

Butterfish (7–12 cm)
rock pools; under stones
near low water

Sand Eel (5–20 cm)
live in shoals in sandy bays;
burrow rapidly in the sand

NO SCALES

Lumpsucker (12–20 cm)
young found in rock pools

eggs

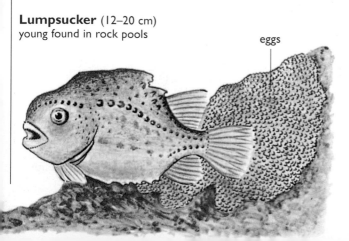

Anemones 46
Artemis shell 32, 59

Barnacle, Acorn 6, 9, 22, 37, 67
Bristletails
Brittlestar 13, 71, 72

Carpet shell 32, 59
Chiton 22, 53, 54
Cockle 7, 8, 30, 57
Coelenterates 44–47
Cowrie 19, 25, 55
Crab group 8, 9, 18, 35, 36, 37, 64, 66, 68–70
Crawfish 38, 68
Crustaceans 9, 11, 36-39, 65–70
Cushion star 13, 72
Cuttlefish 15, 20, 22, 61, 62

Dog cockle 31, 58

Echinoderms 13, 71–73
Eggs 9, 16, 18–21

Fish 10, 16, 19, 21, 40–43, 74–79
Fish eggs 9
Flatfish 40
Food web in the sea 8

Gaper 56, 59

Insects 11, 34, 64

Jellyfish 15, 45, 47

Larvae 9
Limpets 6, 23, 25, 53, 54, 55
Lobster 8, 9, 39, 67

Molluscs 24, 25–33, 52–63
Mussel 8, 30, 57

Necklace shell 20, 27, 55

Octopus 15, 61, 62
Oysters 28, 58

Periwinkle 9
Piddock 29, 56, 58
Pill bug 38, 65, 67
Plankton 8
Prawns 8, 9, 38, 65, 68

Razor shell 29, 56, 59

Sandhoppers 39, 65
Scales, fish
Scallop 29, 57, 58
Sea Anemones 14, 44
  Firs 17, 45, 47

Hare 60, 62
Lemon 62
Mat 17, 46
Mouse 11, 48
Slater 8, 38, 65, 67
Slugs 15, 20, 60, 62
Squirts 16, 72, 73
Star
Shrimp 38, 68
Sponges 16, 47
Starfish 13, 71, 72
Squid 61, 63

Tellin shell 32, 56
Topshells 26, 54
Tower shell 26, 54
Trough shell 33, 58

Urchins 23, 71, 73

Venus shell 32, 59

Wedge shell 33
Whelks 8, 18, 21, 27, 52, 55
Winkles 7, 8, 18, 27, 53, 54, 55
Worms 8, 13, 14, 15, 20, 48–51

Further Reading

Hayward, Peter, Tony Nelson-Smith and Chris Shields, *Collins Pocket Guide to the Seashore of Britain and Northern Europe.* HarperCollins, 1996.
Parker, Steve, *Seashore.* Eyewitness Explorers, Dorling Kindersley, 1994.

A good way to learn more about the animals and plants in your area is to join Wildlife Watch, a club for young people interested in wildlife and the environment. As well as organising activities for its members, Watch produces a national magazine, local newsletters, and many posters and activity packs. Their address is Wildlife Watch, The Green, Witham Park, Waterside South, Lincoln LN5 7JR.